Contents

CROSSING
THE
SOUTHERN
BORDER
Was it worth the risk?

SALLY J. DORAN

Book Cover by Praveen (topbookdesigner)

www.sallyjdoran.com

sallyjdoranauthor@gmail.com

Paperback: 979-8-9924525-0-1

eBook: 979-8-9924525-1-8

First edition 2025

Dedication

I dedicate this novel to my students and others, who with strength, courage, and bravery, have left behind their own country in search of a better life for themselves and their loved ones. Hopefully, they have found it. Precious are the memories forever tucked inside their hearts, and considerable are the lessons learned, the growth achieved.

I would also like to thank Shawna Spencer, Mica Dawn, and Randi Harvey for their valuable edits and suggestions. Especially, I would like to thank my grandson, Nelson James. Without his patience, I may never have finished.

Ms. Sally

Foreword

Why do migrants matter? It is a problem that is more prevalent today than ever. If you were to ask most people today, they probably think they know at least why and where migrants cross the border into the US. They may have an idea—and I thought I did too. But as a teacher and a US citizen, I never stopped to consider the whole picture. What exactly might an undocumented journey entail? Who would ever agree to do this? How do they cross, exactly? Are there life-changing consequences after? The history of migration is the history of how we became who we are today. The answer to these questions is an opportunity to reveal some of the complexities and layers of complicity in migration into the US. Educating the public with an entertaining and timely novel that humanizes the issue is one way to address the problem, especially for young adults who are our leaders of tomorrow.

Based on a true story, Crossing the Southern Border is a poignant exploration of the migrant experience through the eyes of Sofía, a courageous teen from Guatemala fleeing domestic abuse and poverty. This novel attempts to uncover some of the challenges and aspirations of undocumented migrants, uncover the intriguing secrecy behind the smugglers who guide them, and highlight the unforeseen cultural consequences. Authentic stories such as this underscore the social and economic inequalities of those who dare to risk so much to have not just a better future, but a better tomorrow.

This book is important because, of the tens of thousands of similar but untold stories, it captures a written account. This timely narrative not only humanizes the often-misunderstood plight of many migrants, but also invites readers to empathize with diverse cultural backgrounds and engage in critical discussions about immigration; it captures what it is like for brave migrants who dare to cross through countries that do not want them, often unwittingly landing themselves in worse conditions than those they left behind. It is an educational and empathetic resource that will bridge cultural divides and foster compassion in its readership as it incites critical conversations about the future of immigration in this country.

My life-long career in education has made me deeply sympathetic to this issue. Over time, I have become close to my migrant students and that is why as a writer, I wanted to represent their struggles as best I could so that readers become global citizens—ones who are open to multiculturalism and acceptance. I was inspired to write Sofía's story because while reading similar-themed novels of survival journeys in class, I witnessed the impact on my students who generated compassionate discussions of survival, family, choices, and fear of the unknown—followed by superior comprehension of the issues as they developed empathy and critical thinking skills.

Thus, fans who appreciate an emotional survival story featuring brave and determined teens finding success will appreciate Sofía's story. Those on the fence about illegals will learn of the dangerous conditions migrants run from. Moms with tough child separation, family conflicts, betrayal, and domestic abuse benefit from their courage. It educates those curious about coyote operations and cultural identity. Advocates for social justice and the pursuit of the American dream will be enlightened with the details. And fans who participate in book clubs can dive deep into the 10 themes and multitude of questions listed at the end of the book... perhaps broadening mainstream American culture, because immigrants are critical to the functioning of our communities. And that is why migrants and this book matter.

Sally J. Doran

Prologue
A Student with No Voice

School officials typically register the long-standing students first. The late-comers are thrown into whatever class has space leftover. The moment I saw her sitting quietly all the way in the back row, she didn't appear any different from other students I've helped over the years. When I first met Sofía, it was in an elective class in her senior year of high school. She had just arrived a month before and literally spoke no English. She sat somewhat frozen outside her comfort zone, very quiet and unobtrusive, yet stood out among her American classmates with her long dark hair, tannish-colored skin, and black eyes. The school had a small Hispanic population that always fell by the wayside. These migrants tended to be a separate group with a definite set of teachers who welcomed them, and *wanted* to teach them—and a larger set who didn't.

Classes had already started and the busy school counselor placed Sofía, a non-English speaking student, in a 12th grade journalism elective and hoped for the best. I was the English as a Second Language teacher assigned to help her out. I happened to speak Spanish and was surely thrown in for good luck.

Her first assignment was to write a short article for the school newspaper. Each student in the class had to pick school-related topics, get them approved by the teacher, and then write short articles in accordance with the outline already taught. Those important instructions Sofía missed due to complications with her late enrollment. Enthusiastically, I thought we would quickly catch up with the rest of the class by knocking out her overdue assignments with some easy school themes. I suggested we start with writing about how she came to study at Ketcher High School. I felt the rest of the school could learn something about the migrants in their school. Admittedly, I was curious too.

Sofía was stubborn and hesitated to reveal details about herself. I attempted to convince her that those details are always fun for other students to read. After all, this was a newspaper of her peers, and a great way to get to know her. I suggested innocently, *Let's write about how you got here! Let's write about your family and why you left!* She pushed back, not wanting to talk about anything personal. Later that week, I asked around to the other teachers and the counselor to see if they knew anything of her background. *Where is her family? How did she come to be here?* Nobody knew anything. They all remarked how shy she was, shrugged their shoulders, and busily carried on with their school tasks. She remained just another complication for the staff.

Each time I gravitated toward discovering current or past details of home or school life, she withdrew. I could tell she wanted to learn English but somehow, even though she smiled, something held her back. All the while, a desire to unearth answers to my questions grew stronger. Silence was her default.

Over the next several months, after I assisted Sofía to write several short articles on other school "stuff"—which she clearly did not comprehend—I had earned enough trust. Finally, she began to let her guard down. But the number of questions I had for her had grown. *What brought her here? How did she get here? What was life like for her now? Who was she living with? What was school life like for her back in her home country? Is she happy?*

Because the next assignment was due soon, I convinced her that it would be an easy one to complete if I could just interview her. I worried about getting her a passing grade more than anything else. After all, my job as a teacher was to support her in the classroom. I promised we would delete any background information she found too distressing to share if she felt it was too uncomfortable to have published in a school newspaper. It took a lot of effort on my part, but at last, she agreed.

Once Sofía started talking, it was like a flood gate had opened. She began spilling out her story, one she had not shared completely with anyone—not even her family back in Guatemala. She had so much bottled up inside that the Spanish words flew out. She hardly took a breath. It wasn't long before I found myself hanging on every word. Students were moving all around writing and discussing their own articles, and I needed to hear every word Sofía was revealing to me. As I listened to her, I had to hear what she was saying and then mentally interpret her words so quickly that it was giving my brain a workout. Eventually, the noise in the classroom became too much for me. The daily classroom distractions overwhelmed my senses, and I let my co-teacher know Sofía and I would leave the classroom and continue with the assignment elsewhere.

The only place close by was the second-floor girls' bathroom. Once we ducked in, I got out my cell phone to record. Her story was so intense, I didn't want to miss a word. I didn't dare interrupt lest she forget where her emotions were taking her. Students would come in to use the facilities, wash their hands, hit the loud hand-dryer button and leave, all the while I was recording Sofía.

This went on for days. Every day when our journalism class started, Sofía and I would head for the girls' bathroom, and I recorded her speaking her truth, in her own words, in her own language. Some of the students who came to use the bathroom surely looked at us with eyes of judgment, as we stood there next to the mirrors and spoke some foreign language into my cell phone. It must have been an odd sight, and it may have been an intrusion on them, but I didn't care. I needed to understand.

It was indeed challenging to reduce the recordings into a short high school newspaper article that related how Sofía came to study at Ketcher High School, but we did it. We left out 97% of the details and handed in her final draft, knowing that she wouldn't pass her senior year no matter what she produced anyway. She hadn't been in the country long enough to accumulate enough credits to graduate properly.

Yes, we achieved a small goal, but it was at that point I recognized how disheartened I was at the prospect of her future. I realized only a few students would have read her "alien" article with much understanding anyhow. They would probably never notice her among the rest of the migrants who landed in this town. She was seen as foreign, not fitting in. Even if her classmates had learned of her truth like I had, most may not have been as empathetic toward her journey here anyway. The world was experiencing one of the greatest migrations over the border than ever before, while her school community was in the middle of school debates over the sharply divided presidential race for Camp-Trump or Camp-Biden. Needless to say, Ketcher

High School expressed its limited diversity as one reflected in a tapestry of flannel shirts, dirt bikes, guns, pickup trucks, and the construction of walls. She didn't have a chance.

When Sofía's short article was published on-line that week for the entire school to read, it didn't seem to interest her, but I felt rather defeated. It was I who had convinced her to release that small part of her story to her peers. *What would they think? Would they feel differently toward her? Would they understand?* I wrongly imagined she felt the same as I did. Surprisingly, Sofía wasn't phased—it was just another assignment completed for a class she didn't comprehend, a language she didn't speak, and ultimately was not going to pass.

But I couldn't let her story out of my mind. It haunted me to remember back in the girls' bathroom, the intensity of her journey, how emotional she had become, and how the tears flowed. Recollecting the part that would change her life forever, she cried out to me as I recorded her story: "But I caught the baby, I caught the baby, I caught the baby!" It isn't every migrant's story, only one of thousands who have ventured to uproot their lives to cross a border in hopes of something better. This is Sofía's story, a glimpse into her destiny and the chain of events that produced struggles, risks and a few lucky opportunities. It reflects the pursuit everyone in the chain was after, no matter how small the link, no matter the obstacle, no matter a six-foot wall where someone could catch a baby.

The Journey

San Marcos, Guatemala → La Mesilla → Frontera de México → Guadalajara, Jalisco → San Luis Potosí → Sonora → Nogales → AZ., EE.UU.

Chapter One

Young Love Starts the Journey

Q: What are the statistics on domestic violence in Central America?

A: El Salvador and Guatemala rank first and second, respectively, in rates of homicide against children and adolescents globally. In Guatemala, every 46 minutes a new case of sexual violence is reported, but the number of incidents is likely much higher as many go unrecorded. Gender-based violence remains one of the most significant yet overlooked drivers of out-migration across Central America and the broader region.

They say that young people today naturally have so many choices and opportunities in life. "Take charge, be in control, voice your opinion," they're encouraged. "Dream big! Live life!

Reach for the Stars!" But that's not exactly how it was for Sofía. In fact, none of that was true for her. Her choice to leave wasn't her choice at all. Through the immense love her mother had for her, she was told she *had* to go and leave her entire life behind. And through the love and respect she had for her mother and sister, the decision to leave was graciously accepted, no ifs, ands, or buts.

Sofía's mother, Betina, had fifteen siblings: twelve girls and three boys. This was a typical Guatemalan family that relied heavily on hard work, luck, and prayers. Three of Betina's siblings left Guatemala and made it to the United States: Martina, who ended up in Ketcher, New York; Brenda who somehow came to live in New Jersey; and a brother Cecilio, whose journey landed him in North Carolina. The rest remained in Guatemala. None of the details of how or why were ever discussed.

Sofía grew up in the small town of San Marcos. Her mom was never married to her father. He had another wife and children in a nearby town, yet he came around every so often to check on them and keep them hoping for a better life. Betina had five daughters with him. Sofía was the youngest.

Besides issues of crime, drug trafficking, and civil instability, Guatemala had almost a 60 percent poverty rate. Unfortunately, Sofía's family was part of the statistics. Until she was five, all her siblings and mother slept in a tiny, cramped room at their grandfather's modest house made of sticks and a thatched roof with a dirt floor. There were no brick, tile, or wooden floors. Being near the equator, it was not uncommon in the poorer sections of any town for families to sleep on dirt floors, as they looked for ways to cool down from the squelching heat of the constant sun.

Even in 2017, Sofía's family had to go daily to the nearby river to get water. At night, they used candles to light the way if they needed to go to the bathroom. Eventually, her dad built her mom a small two-room house that had a floor, water, electricity, a very small refrigerator, and a coveted small television. Only people with money lived in houses that had more than two rooms with separate quarters for all family members. Only the wealthy had a separate bathroom and appliances. But as a proud head of household, Betina took her children to church every Sunday. Religious commitment was a high priority and daily prayers were tradition in her family.

Sofía slept in a single room with three beds: She and two of her sisters slept in one bed, her two older sisters in another, and her mom in the third. That's just the way it was. However humble it may have been, she always felt the comfort surrounded by her family.

When Sofía's life-changing story began, she was thirteen and a half years old. One of her sisters, Carmen, had just turned fifteen. The problem arose when Carmen secretly began dating

Gunner, who was now twenty-seven years old—almost twice her age—against her family's wishes. They hid their relationship because of the obvious age difference and because Gunner had earned himself a negative reputation in their small town. Gangs were everywhere. It was normal to learn of domestic violence and murder. It was an increasingly unsafe place where they lived, especially for innocent young girls who were easily disposed of. Even babies were kidnapped, held for ransom, or never seen again.

Gunner, a nice-looking guy had countless girlfriends in the past. He had been running around with many women and had no real incentive to settle down. He had no children and no emotional ties from any previous relationship. He was spoiled having no siblings to share affection or wealth. His mother and father were divorced. His father was a very abusive alcoholic. That is where Gunner learned about abuse. He grew up seeing his dad come home drunk and beat his mother for the slightest thing. Witnessing his mom with bruises and swollen facial features was normal. The yelling and name-calling was an every-day event. Money was tight and happy times were scarce. Holidays and family gatherings were always festive but fake. Inside, everyone was bleeding from despair.

Young girls like Sofía's sister Carmen felt flattered that men would be attracted to her; she didn't know any better and hid his flirtatious advances from her siblings and especially her mother. It was just the cultural norm that older Latin men went after the younger girls. Amongst men, they got away with it as being a natural thing to do. But amongst women, they grew up resenting it, when eventually, they learned how their innocence and dignity had been swindled from them.

With foresight and wisdom, Betina had warned her young daughters about men. Lectures and warnings were common from parents, school, and church, about chastity, about being virtuous, and being safe. But young kids will do what young kids do. No matter how purposeful, the sermons and lectures fell on deaf ears. Many young kids, like Carmen, ignored the warning signs they were taught and were destined to repeat the cycle.

Sofía sensed there was something not right, but she was still too young to realize what was really going on. During the conversations she and her sister had in the bed they shared at night, she was aware that Carmen behaved differently as she talked about her secret meetings with Gunner. Although Sofía suspected there was more to the story, Carmen insisted she and Gunner were 'just friends.' She didn't know how to voice her thoughts exactly, because she rather enjoyed seeing Carmen so happy...so she quietly listened.

Beyond any doubt, Gunner knew how old Carmen was. He persuaded her to hide their relationship from her family. Carmen hated to acknowledge that her mom never would agree to their dating in the first place. Although it had crossed her mind about the anti-contraception methods available and legal, she knew they were rarely offered to teenagers in Guatemala. Some organizations offered classes about pregnancies, but it was still rare for a younger person to go to a hospital or pharmacy and ask for a contraceptive. In fact, it would have been scandalous. And one day, through manipulation, lies, and a lot of self-importance, Gunner took advantage of her, and she became pregnant.

Carmen couldn't keep it a secret for long and confided in her dearest sister, Sofía. Once more, Sofía just listened. As she thought of her sister's future—the lack of security, lack of money, the lack of resources to care for a baby, their age difference—she accepted what Carmen was telling her, but because she didn't want to see Carmen stop smiling, she remained silent. Carmen didn't worry about the finances. She knew the hospital costs were covered when women had babies in her town, so there would be no cost. She also knew that in most Latin countries abortion is illegal. It was unheard of for a woman to get an abortion, so that route never occurred to her.

As in all small Latin towns, everybody knew everybody. These two families had first been acquainted with each other years earlier when Gunner's mom dated Carmen's Uncle Cecilio after Gunner's biological dad left them for another woman. Their brief romance didn't last long, and Reina married another man, Abel. Together, Reina's family and his new step-father Abel founded and managed a small shoe store. They encouraged Gunner to work there. He didn't like what he did and was often bored. His mother let him slack off most of the time. Of course, girls, even nice girls like Carmen, were attracted to him because of his bad-boy charm. The thought that he had money wasn't bad either.

This time around, unlike her abusive first husband, Reina had married a weak man whom she could boss around. Although she was a survivor of abuse herself, Reina had become someone who abuses as a way to deal with her own complex trauma. She had become a controlling matriarch who was very attached to her son. This new dynamic with a less-authoritative step-father only inflated Gunner's sense of power. Reina and Gunner looked down on Carmen's family because Betina had never actually been married to Carmen's father. Marriage was considered like having status, a way to announce to the world that you are somebody, that you matter to someone. This made Reina and Gunner feel empowered, like they were better and socially more prominent.

Carmen was just two months along when she confessed to her mom that she had become pregnant. When Betina discovered the truth about the pregnancy and her daughter's ties with an unscrupulous gang member, she was disappointed in Carmen but kept her reactions loving and light-hearted; she welcomed the thought of a grand-baby. Inside though, Betina was destroyed. She knew all too well what the future held for Carmen, yet she respected her daughter's decision to carry on with Gunner and prayed for the best. They all prayed for the unborn baby. Sofía felt the shift in the air. She knew their lives were changing but said nothing for fear of the unknown. They continued to go to church every Sunday and pray to God. They included prayers to Saint James, the Patron Saint of Guatemala, also one of Jesus's Twelve Apostles. He would surely help them. They counted on all the blessings the Heavens would send them.

When Reina found out that her son had gotten a 'pitiful' girl pregnant, she ordered Carmen to come live with them immediately. No son of hers was going to have an unwed girl carrying his baby. That was disgraceful and distasteful to the community, one where Reina needed the appearance of power and social status, complete with tradition. Gunner thought this was great, since now he had a live-in maid who would serve him and have dinner ready for him when he came home from the shoe store...and other perhaps degenerate adventures. Instantly, he became even more controlling. He decided he didn't want Carmen to go out or have friends anymore, and he didn't want her visiting her own family while his mom began preparations for a wedding. Reina, building resentment, had to pay for the celebration because it was clear that Carmen's family did not have any money.

Isolated from her family, confined and lonely, Carmen's life as she knew it before was forever changed. Betina only agreed to let her young daughter go live in Gunner's house under the condition they would be getting married. Sofía was heartbroken. She tried to focus on the future when the baby would be born. She and Carmen had been so close, raised almost as twins. They missed each other terribly.

As soon as Carmen moved in, she was ordered to do all the cooking and cleaning, like a servant. Gunner's mother was very mean the way she spoke to Carmen. She was beyond disappointed that her son had impregnated a "worthless young girl from a low-class, unsuitable family with nothing to offer." Reina often made comments to Carmen that she "indeed came from an indigent family because of the many sisters she had, and that her mom was never married to her dad." Carmen tried her best to follow the rules in her new living situation while she attempted, without success, to assist Reina plan her wedding to Gunner.

Ingrained in the culture, Latin guys like Gunner were raised to act 'machista' and condescending toward women. Men, especially those in gangs, tended to beat their women and threaten them with violence and guns. Carmen, scared and secluded, began to see signs of this but felt she had no one to talk to. She really missed the nightly talks with Sofía. She was aware that all too often, adverse domestic incidents resulted from the disobedience of young women. Carmen was learning first-hand that this abuse typically didn't get reported, and even if it were, the authorities would see this customary behavior as normal and easily dismiss it. She wondered how she would ever be able to contact someone for help if she needed it. Unfortunately, with so many other issues, she concluded domestic violence would not be on the radar of the Guatemalan Police.

Gunner was often manipulative toward Carmen. He threatened to kick her out of the house and essentially kidnap their little baby once born, if she didn't do exactly as he said. His favorite words to call her were "whore" and "no-good wench." He raised his hand to her many times, but she never let him hit her...at least not in the face. Sadly, Carmen knew she would become brainwashed over time, only to repeat the cycle if she didn't find a way to speak up and get out.

When Carmen was about four months pregnant, exactly one day before the wedding— as if in pure spite, Reina called it off. She had become so disgusted at the idea of Carmen becoming part of her family, she refused to let her only son marry a pregnant sixteen-year-old. Reina declared in one of her tirades that "this poor girl would *not* marry her son." In reality, she did not want an ingrate to receive an inheritance from the shoe store under any circumstances. And so, they were never married.

Traditionally, the groom's-side paid for all the wedding essentials. Even though Reina lost what money she had spent in preparation for the big day, she was content that she kept her kingdom in tact and they didn't get married...but she would make Carmen earn her keep. Alone and ashamed, Carmen didn't have the heart or the courage to tell her mother why her future mother-in-law called it off. Instead, she called her older sister Alma, and asked her to break the news to their mom. Betina, as expected, was furious. Her dreams for her daughter were destroyed. As Carmen expected, her mother felt deceived and extremely disappointed. Now, Carmen would be an unmarried young girl with no future to speak of, living in a house as a domestic slave to their whims.

Gunner wasn't upset at all that his wedding was called off. He was amused. However, the animosity increased between the families in no time. Sofía had witnessed it all unfold. She stood back and watched as her mother's anger grew. Sofía, although confused, felt she was too young to know what to do, say or to have an opinion yet. But she knew one day she would speak up and let the world know how unfair her sister had been treated.

Even though deep-down Carmen knew this situation she found herself in was all wrong and going nowhere, but for the love of her unborn baby, she continued to live for many more months in Gunner's house, hoping the situation would fix itself once born. She thought she was doing the right thing by staying with Gunner. She thought he would change.

Chapter Two

Stood Up at the Altar

Q: Which is more painful: Getting hit by your boyfriend or

escaping because of your boyfriend?

A: Intentions are everything.

Over the next several months, Carmen tried her best to please Gunner and his mother. Because Gunner's house was close enough to get to on foot, Betina would find reasons to pass by their house whenever she could to check on her daughter. Reina would answer the door and tell Betina that Carmen wasn't home. Betina would go back to the house crying. She suspected that her daughter was suffering from abuse.

Carmen was still young—almost seventeen-years-old now. Spending close to two years with Gunner had made her so vulnerable and impressionable. The few and far between times she did speak to her mother, she didn't dare tell her what was really happening. But, between motherly instincts and intuition, Betina knew her daughter was in trouble.

The arguments weren't as explosive when Gunner and Carmen first began living together. But as the miserable situation droned on, the quarreling in Gunner's house escalated. No one was happy. Life was hard. The negativity, the tension, and the stress of it all was unbearable...most of the time. Little by little, discussions became loud verbal battles, and the physicality grew. Alcohol was always involved. Any discussion of money was a sure trigger. Name-calling, belittling, and disparaging remarks were enough to knock down anyone's self-esteem. By then, threats of kidnapping the baby and Carmen's insignificance, even disposal, were a daily theme.

The night they had their biggest fight, Carmen didn't have dinner on the table when Gunner got home from the shoe store. They easily fought in front of the baby and in front of Reina and her husband. Carmen had reached her breaking point. Gunner yelled at Carmen, cussing his usual degrading names, calling her a "lazy bitch." As expected, Reina agreed with her son and called her a "slow-moving, indolent deadbeat." Abel sat there sipping his Guaro liquor; he didn't look up and didn't dare say a word. At one point, Reina grabbed Carmen's arm and scolded her for what she considered an unkempt house—not fit for the likes of her. Carmelita cried out the whole time. The domestic abuse had become routine exposure to thirteen-month-old Carmelita.

Meanwhile, Gunner had told Carmen many times to never leave the house. He made her clean every nook and cranny and complained if he thought something was out of order. She was responsible for cooking him breakfast, lunch, and dinner every day, in addition to caring for Carmelita. His treatment of her was like a personal servant instead of the mother of his child. Fearful and scared, Carmen never verbalized what she felt inside. She never threatened to leave or gave him an indication that she would leave, even though every cell of her body wondered why. Gunner never suspected she would.

That night, Carmen remained diligently in the kitchen doing the dishes and cleaning up. Reina and her husband had customarily attended church several times a week right after dinner. Carmen waited until they stepped out to go to church at 7:30 PM. Gunner left soon after to go out drinking and carousing with his buddies. Carmen dashed into the bedroom and pulled out the documents and paperwork she had secretly organized during the day. She needed records from Carmelita's pediatrician and her birth certificate. A small bag was all she needed to pack Carmelita's clothes. This escape had been brewing in her mind for weeks now.

Soon after Reina left, Carmen once again called her older sister. As fast as she could get the words out, she explained the problems she had with Gunner—that she needed to escape and go back home before they returned. Once again, she asked Alma to break it to Betina. She didn't yet have the courage to tell her mother herself. Carmen felt like she had failed after all the compounding truths her mom had warned her about.

As soon as Alma confessed to their mom that Carmen pleaded to come home, Betina wasted no time getting up and ran out the front door to help her daughter carry the baby and her things back home. Her suspicions were confirmed. They didn't own a car. None needed. As fast as she could, she ran the several street blocks to Gunner's house, praying to God and Saint James the entire way. Carmen stood there waiting nervously at the front door. They greeted each other with their eyes and, without hesitation, Carmen handed the baby over to Betina. Carmen picked up the few bags she had to her name and carried them back to their house. As swift as a rescue could be—mother, daughter, and baby—they picked up the pace to reach home without words, without blame, and without regrets.

Once home, Betina locked the doors, closed all the windows, and asked Carmen a million questions. Carmen chose not to reveal everything just yet. She didn't want to upset her mother too much, as she had been hiding their troublesome relationship for over two years. Down the road, in much calmer times, if ever, Carmen figured she would confess just how badly she was treated. Betina had warned her, lectured her, and had given her best effort to avoid having any of her daughters repeat the cycle. Feeling guilty and ashamed, Carmen knew her mom was not ready to face reality so soon.

Sofía sat and listened to their conversation. She heard the prayers and witnessed her mom's faith many times before when times got tough. Being just one year younger than Carmen, she didn't know what to think. Of course, she was sad and would side with her mother's and sister's point of view over whatever Gunner's family might have said or done. Her heart broke for Carmen, and she thought about how awful it must have been to be stood up at the altar and four months pregnant. Her mother's anguish toward Carmen's situation deeply affected Sofía: it informed her of the importance of following rules. Betina was disappointed and disillusioned that now her youngest daughter had to witness this distressing situation. She was determined to never let this happen to her youngest, Sofía.

A temporary small back room was fixed to hide Carmen and the baby following their return home. Betina was relieved to get her daughter back and to see the baby laugh. For the next fifteen days, Gunner would knock on their door, but Betina refused to let him in the house. He knew they were there but didn't make a big deal about it...yet. He was relieved not to have to fight every night. He enjoyed the break, although he was not totally convinced Carmen and the baby would be back in his own house soon.

It was in those fifteen days that Betina made her plans. Every few days, another knock. Gunner would show up, demanding to get Carmen and the baby. Sofía would help Carmen entertain the baby as they tried hard to remain silent. Baffled, he couldn't understand why she wanted to be with her mother.

Over and over, his pride got the better of him as he banged on the door, "Let me in, get me Carmelita! She belongs at my house! You stole my daughter!" He continued threats of an Amber Alert, legal action, and occasionally something worse. He repeated, "Carmelita has a right to know her father and be in his life!"

Still, never once did he take accountability for his or his mother's actions. He stressed that it was all Betina's fault, that if it were not for her, they would "happily still be together." Almost sermon-like, he painted a picture of himself as a hard worker at the shoe store and his shoe-store money to try and change her mind.

But Betina would remind him of his and his mother's delusional, controlling, and aggressive behavior toward her and the baby. Gunner really believed his own lies and deceit. Betina would respond, "She's not only your daughter. She's my granddaughter too!"

It was a small town and word of strained situations always gets around. Up to this point, Betina and Gunner's mother had tolerated each other. Once things turned scandalous, there was nothing either mother could do to change the situation or make the past go away. Betina was not letting her daughter return. Threats from Gunner to kidnap *his* baby fell on Betina's deaf ears. She grew increasingly afraid for the future of Carmen and baby Carmelita.

Inevitably, Betina found the courage to dredge up memories of her siblings and how they had escaped similar situations in Guatemala searching for a better life. Several of Betina's sisters and a brother had left years earlier and found their way across the border, presumably happy now. She recognized that this was the moment to stop the madness and save both daughters and a baby from a dreadful cycle of the same. She convinced herself that Carmen needed to get away before it was too late, and Sofía would be her support. She reminded them how good God was, and with faith and prayers, all would be resolved. With a heavy heart, Betina knew the pattern had to end. Her best solution landed on getting Carmen far away from Gunner, and that meant starting a new life before Gunner and his family did any more damage to their lives.

Betina was a mother whose upbringing and past made her bound and determined to get her daughters away to safety. It came to the point where there were no more options left to consider. She thought of sending them away as their last hope that another generation would not repeat the cycle and finally break the chain. Betina saw herself in Carmen. Her only wish now was to get them to safety and spare her last daughter Sofía any more of the unhealthy events she had been witnessing.

Betina unselfishly introduced the idea that perhaps Carmen should leave Guatemala and go to her Aunt Martina's house in New York. It didn't take much to convince Carmen that in the United States, she would find an abundance of opportunities. There, Gunner could never get away with kidnapping their baby girl. She was desperate and afraid that if Gunner's anger got the better of him, he would carry out worse physical threats, and the rest of the family would never see Carmelita again. Betina feared that if Carmen didn't free herself now, she would be in an abusive relationship forever with no chance for a better future. It was all she knew. She did not want her daughter to end up like herself, unmarried, poor, and emotionally and physically depleted. If she could help it, Betina would *not* let history repeat itself.

It was a given that Carmen couldn't make the trip alone. Betina knew—everyone knew—how dangerous the journey to cross the border was. She called all her children together for a serious family meeting. When everyone arrived, they took a seat at the small kitchen table. She looked around at her other grown children. Betina had three older daughters: Enid, a store clerk; Sara, a secretary; and Alma, a nurse. Only two were married and their relationships were questionably healthy. Poor and struggling but living close by, they were nevertheless Betina's pride and joy. The only two girls left were Carmen and Sofía.

As Betina's plan came together, she knew it wouldn't be long before Sofía could fall into the same fate as Carmen. If letting one daughter go was hard, two was even harder. Betina convinced herself as the saying went, "You can't read the directions from inside the jar." Carmen and the baby needed someone to help them. She took a deep breath and without hesitation, declared that Sofía would accompany Carmen as soon as they found the chance to depart from their little town in Guatemala. With sorrowful eyes, Betina looked at Sofía and explained that she *had* to do this for Carmen, her baby, and for herself. They had to fight for their freedom even though at this time she may not fully understand why.

Sofía felt she had no choice and wouldn't say anything even if she did. It stung. It was a done deal. At first, she felt very sad. As the family meeting continued, Sofía's head spun. *But I don't know English!* She knew that to leave her country, the differences in languages would be an astronomical hurdle for her. As she tried to process the information thrown at her, her biggest, most immediate fear was leaving her mother, her traditions—the only environment she ever knew, and her friends. Just the thought of communicating with people in English made her panic. *I don't know English!* A million thoughts of fear barged into her brain, as she became overwhelmed by the picture that was unfolding.

Oddly enough, Sofía found herself simultaneously entertaining thoughts about what it would be like to explore speaking with people who were different. Curiously, just for a few seconds, she allowed herself to consider what it must be like to speak in English and perhaps make new friends. She tried her best to look on the bright side as the conflicting thoughts of fear and curiosity bounced around in her head. Her sweaty palms and beating heart reflected a whirlwind of emotions that tingled throughout her body. She missed her mom already.

At first, she tried only to think about what it meant to respect her mother's wishes and help her sister, and *not* think about what it would be like for herself. It was hard because every now and then, visions of foreign places flashed in her head. The sounds of people speaking a foreign language crept into her thoughts. She repeated to herself, *I don't know how to speak English!* But she trusted her mother. Sofía resolved that her mom's decision reflected her hopes for a better life for them, even though they all knew what it meant—soon they would be separated.

There wasn't much talk after that family meeting besides bowing their heads to pray. That was it. Sofía willfully accepted the plan and to follow the rules that were put into motion. Time was of the essence. It was time for Sofía to look forward and not back.

Chapter Three

Decisions & Plans: Which Route?

Q. Does your mom always know what is best?

A. Maybe.

They had less than a month to complete the fast-developing plan of departure from San Marcos. With help from the Patron Saint of Guatemala in their prayers, they hoped to arrive safely at Aunt Martina's place in New York. They had precious few days to ward off Gunner and set the girls off to a better life.

Many questions arose. Alma asked anxiously, "*How* can we do this and who will help them?"

Enid asked softly, "Where will you get the money?"

Carmen asked, "Do you really think we can get through this journey safely, with a baby, all the way from Central America, through Mexico and into the United States?"

Alma looked at her mother and challenged her, "Is this an undertaking that two very young girls with a baby can handle?"

Carmen wanted to know what happens after. She asked, "What will become of our lives once there?" "Is our aunt ready to sponsor us?"

Sofía preferred to stay silent as she listened to everyone else. Her thoughts told her there are just two things this plan sounded like: dangerous and possibly deadly. She was too young to know all the specifics. She hadn't contemplated her future before this. Not wanting to let the others see how scared and frightened she was, she remained quiet as she asked herself, *What will become of me? What dangerous things will we face along the way? Can I handle them? I don't know any English at all! How can I do this?* But she knew in her heart there was no turning back. Never once did she think to say no to her family.

As Sofía played with the baby, she overheard her mom and sisters discussing what had happened to Uncle Cecilio, Betina's brother. He had made the journey into the States a few years before. He could have chosen the more popular option, to go hidden in a large truck and most likely get caught and sent back. His other option was to go on foot through the Mexican desert. It was much more dangerous but less complicated to go through the desert because one could travel with fewer people. Unfortunately, Uncle Cecilio chose to go on foot and got lost due to the brutal conditions of the desert. He spent fifteen days alone there on a path that should have taken around five or six days. Fifteen days was a long time to be lost in a desert! *It was a miracle that he survived. But he made it.*

She heard them agree on the need for a cell phone for communication and emergencies. During their uncle's migration, Betina recalled that on occasion, "He would find ways to communicate and describe what he was going through. Having a cell phone is probably the most important thing the girls will need."

Sofía listened to their conversations but didn't dare interrupt them; her job was to keep Carmelita occupied. She couldn't help imagining how brutal his journey was and thought how wise to bring enough snacks and a secretly hidden knife—hidden for defense should he need it.

"At some point," Betina continued, "Luckily he ran into someone else who was also lost in the desert, and they stayed together. There was no cell phone coverage in the desert. He saw lots of poisonous spiders, snakes, and wolves. At night, he covered himself up with tree branches, for the nights got cold. He used the sticks for protection and to hide from immigration police who may have spotted him. When your uncle finally reached the border, he met up with a group of total strangers who happened to make it there at the same time, and he slipped into the US with them."

He did it, she thought again.

Sofía remembered the details. All those stories frightened her, but she never said a word. *His entire journey took one and a half months. Forty-five days is considered an abnormally long time for a person to get to the border! Normal journeys on foot through the desert should last about ten to fifteen days. How long will my journey last?*

Betina did not want that for her daughters. She conceded that going through the desert, possibly getting lost, and not knowing what to do was not for them, so she decided they would have to go the other way and risk the routine police checks.

The plan was unfolding and in process. Next step, find a coyote to escort the girls to the Mexican border and into the United States. Sofía overheard her mom say, "I know I will have to pay these guys a hefty fee to get them across. Some coyotes charge more, some less; some take one route, others take another, easier route. We just needed to find the safest one for them."

Carmen remained in hiding from her now ex-boyfriend while Betina went to work to find a person to guide them safely to the border. As luck would have it, a close friend of Uncle Cecilio got them in touch with the same coyote as he had. Within hours, a dark-haired, rather short man about 45 years-old showed up at their door. Betina invited him to sit down at the kitchen table. She wasted no time asking when he could bring the three girls and how much it would cost.

The coyote needed the details about the girls' ages. He negotiated, "If you are older, it's more money. Younger, less money." Then explained, "Older people tend to get sent back more, and they will have to try again. You'll have up to three tries to cross, so the cost is higher. But the younger children tend to go through the border the first try, so they cost less." This coyote recognized how hard it was for Betina's family to gather up a large sum of money. But paying his set fee would give them up to three chances to get through the border. He said he would attempt two more times if the girls failed the first time around. However, if after the third time it didn't work, he would keep all the money.

"Here are your two options:"

"One: Take the route through the Mexican desert and into the United States. A good chunk would be on foot by a small number of migrants at a time. The girls would probably be in a tractor-trailer, locked-in at times. They would definitely face some danger against the elements of a desert, and random men who could rape them. Sometimes the men they might encounter could shoot them down for whatever possessions they thought the girls might be carrying. Reaching the border this way might be easier in many ways for male adults since men don't carry much with them. Men can defend themselves against attackers in most cases, and this route leads to a place where they wouldn't have to deal with much border patrol once they arrive. Or,

Two: Go the route that avoids a lot of the desert dangers...but the girls would have to ride in vehicles with a larger number of people while changing modes of transportation often. The girls would have to be disguised as Mexicans and/or hidden in trucks, vans, and buses throughout the journey until they reach the US border. The greatest risk this way lies with the Mexican police patrols along the way which stop to check *all* the vehicles day and night. This is where the girls would get turned back if they are discovered hidden in a vehicle or suspected to be a migrant. Eventually, when they get to the border crossing, they would be dropped off near it. They would have to go on their own through usual broken holes in the border wall, and then deal with the US Immigration Officers who wait on the other side. Again, there's the possibility they would be sent right back as soon as they made it over."

As the coyote non-nonchalantly finished his thoughts, he smiled and said, "Those are the risks to consider. Another group is leaving soon, so you need to decide."

The risks of either option were terrorizing. Betina tried to process the ideas that random men would be lurking around her girls, AND the threat of rape, AND the possibility of being shot for their possessions, AND having to take a baby across the desert, AND being locked in a tractor trailer. The perils were staggering. They ALL sounded awful. But it didn't take more than five seconds to think about it and she chose the second option.

"First, it seems an easier route from what my brother endured, and second, because the girls are younger there is a much better chance of getting processed through once they reach the other side."

Once Betina got the essential information she needed, she told the coyote she would take out a loan to pay the cost. She ran the different scenarios through her mind as she reminded herself, "It's not so unusual, word would get around fast, so time is ticking." She trusted that it was pretty common that if you get sent back, you get a second and third chance with the same money. It was a lot of money, but Betina trusted the plan. She believed in her daughters' abilities to find their way. Even though it had been years and years since she knew much about her sister in New York, she trusted her as family. She envisioned a better life for them—a future far from Guatemala. There was one last thing on her to-do list: she needed to share the plan with the girls and ensure they were on board.

It was time to have a heart-to-heart talk with Sofía and Carmen. By then, Sofía was almost sixteen, Carmen seventeen, and the baby was just thirteen months old. This was a long shot, a hope, and a prayer, but she felt it was worth the risk. Betina kept her words transparent and to the point. She explained, "If you travel the first option, through the desert, you could cross the border with less resistance but most likely you'd travel the entire way on foot. Not good. It would be very risky; many problems could arise for two young girls and a baby, not to mention how much more dangerous. And if you went the other way, you would arrive most likely in a truck or bus, but with the stronger possibility of being stopped and sent back by either the Mexican Border Patrol or the US immigration who would be waiting for you on either side of the border."

The girls looked at each other and froze. Betina could see the fear in their eyes. Carmen studied Sofía's face and asked, "Are you sure you're OK to leave here and go with me?"

"Yes, mom thinks it is best so I can help you and the baby when we get to the US." Sofía responded with hesitation, "But once we are there, can we help bring mom to the US too?"

Carmen smiled with a sigh of relief and said, "Of course! We will bring mom as soon as we can."

Betina reminded them, "Imagine the struggle you are leaving behind, and the freedom you will find in your futures." She promised them, like her sisters and brother who lived there now,

"The US was a paradise, full of wealth and opportunities for young ladies." Betina advised them as others had told her, "The American Dream is real, and it is your last hope." With tears in her eyes she declared, "Yes, I want a better future for my children, but for now I'm hoping for a *safe tomorrow*." The choice was clear.

A few days later, Betina contacted the coyote. He asked for 100,000 quetzales or $12,949.27 American dollars for the three of them. He required a deposit of half the amount up front. The arrangement was to pay the other half when they arrived at the border.

Soon after Betina managed to take out the loan. Coming up with that kind of money was a monumental task for sure, but Sofía noted how quickly the chain of events unfolded. She was amazed as she heard her mom comment how easy it was to get the loan. *Even the bankers are a part of this plan...it's all falling into place so easily.*

As she briefly met again with the coyote, Betina thought about the risks of handing over half of the money—and her daughters—to a stranger. She worried but had confidence that it was not typical for a coyote to run off with the money and not fulfill his arrangement. She had heard about many people getting sent back, so she had faith her girls could try again without another loan. "With that agreement," the coyote said, "I'll call you when I'm ready to leave."

The anticipation filled everyone with anxiety and stress. Sofía was nervous. She couldn't sleep. She cried hidden tears while she cycled through lots of emotions of fear, curiosity, and hope. Both sisters were processing the separation that would come, as they tried their hardest not to think about it. They didn't know if it would happen today, tonight, tomorrow, next week...but soon.

The day finally came. Betina was alone in the supermarket when her cell phone rang. Her heart pounded. It was a Saturday. They were to leave on Monday, February 6, 2017. She knew everyone's life was about to change forever. The supermarket was not far from their house. She called the oldest daughter, Enid, to tell the girls she'd be home shortly.

"Tell them all to wait for me in the kitchen."

Enid told everyone to wait around the kitchen table because their mother was about to return from the supermarket with some news. Carmen grabbed Carmelita and ran to the first chair she saw. Sofía and the other sisters stood waiting for their mother to arrive. When she walked through the front door of the house to meet them, she reached her arms out and gave them a group hug. She said, "You're leaving on Monday."

Gunner still didn't know a thing.

Preparation for Departure

Q: How do you prepare to leave your country?

A: With a heart full of memories, comfortable shoes and a Mexican dialect.

Sofía's heart pounded. *What's going to happen to us on Monday?* For the first time she cried in front of her mother and sisters. They all cried and prayed together, just as Betina had taught them.

The tears flowed among all the women for nearly an entire hour. Once they stopped, they made a list of the things they needed for the journey, and off Betina went to the town store. She bought a backpack for Carmen and Sofía, comfortable shoes, and even shoes for Carmelita. Because of their uncle's experience, they thought they knew what they would need: enough snacks, a light jacket or sweatshirt, money, a cell phone, a few prayers, and a lot of luck. Necessities for the baby would be needed: crackers, cookies, granola bars, water, diapers, milk, and three changes of clothing.

In a small sack, the girls fit a small baby blanket, a couple of sweaters and two tops as well. Next, both Carmen and Sofía carefully ripped their underwear to sew Mexican money in the seams. The coyote warned their mother they couldn't carry cash anywhere else. It all had to be hidden. The coyote would supply each with false Mexican identification. Sofía memorized her aunt's phone number in New York and wrote it in pen underneath her arm…just in case. They agreed adding minutes on a cell phone from Guatemala to the US was an additional but necessary expense. The cell phone would be their lifeline to their mother. Like their uncle, they relied on phones for safety and peace of mind whenever, if ever, they had an opportunity to connect—no matter how costly.

Sunday morning, the coyote called with instructions for their next step. He reminded them, "There are two borders to cross. First, you'll need to prepare to cross the border of Guatemala into Mexico, then eventually, you'll cross the Mexican border into the US."

The coyote had rounded up his latest group of migrants and directed them to meet at a certain hotel near the border of Guatemala, in a town called La Mesia. It was a simple and unsuspecting place, yet held great importance for the travelers.

Their lives as they knew them would separate there. Betina understood she may never see her daughters and granddaughter again once they crossed into Mexico. She needed to see them off and spend their last night together. To make the trip special, Betina rented a van so all her children could travel together comfortably to see them off and hug them one last time. They drove just under six long hours and 300 miles from San Marcos to the Guatemala-Mexican border in La Mesia.

That night, as the new group of migrants gathered for the first time in the lobby of a shabby hotel, the coyote wasted no time summoning them together to teach them some useful tips for success. He passed around a sheet of paper with a list of things they each should know and be prepared to do during the trip. It was crucial that they understood how to handle possible interrogation questions by the Mexican border patrol; if the patrols suspected they were a migrant trying to cut through Mexico to get into the US, they would stop them right there, possibly arrest them, and, without hesitation, send them back.

The coyote warned them: "If you're detained, the Mexican officer of immigration will try and trick you by asking, *What Department are you from?* In Guatemala, we call our local counties 'departmentos' whereas in Mexico, they call them 'estados.' The terminology difference is *really* important. Depending on your reply—'departmento' or 'estado'—the police will know immediately if you are from Mexico. If travelers were indeed true Mexicans, they would have answered the question in their dialect and vocabulary. *Is that clear?"*

This shocked Sofía as she tried to piece together what he was teaching them. Everyone had to memorize these facts to make a successful trip. She felt terrified. *How will I ever remember so many items on this fact sheet and not mess things up for the others? I don't know if I can do this! What if I say the wrong thing? What if I get sent back, or get separated from my sister?* Laser-focused, she studied them over and over again.

It was now Monday, February 6th, 2017. At 4:00 PM, the coyote gave a quick three-tap knock on each migrant's hotel door, summoning them to come out again. It was another strategic pep talk in the hotel lobby. Sofía looked around. It was the first time she had really noticed the other people. They came from all over Central America: Honduras, El Salvador, Costa Rica, Guatemala, and Nicaragua. She was still in a daze. It happened so fast. She asked Carmen under her breath, "Are you ready for this?"

Carmen didn't respond. She only nodded her head, "Yes."

They listened intently.

"Always stay in the same group," demanded the coyote, "because you can easily get lost." He went on, "Remember, if an official from Mexico says to get off the bus, we can't say 'no' because we are from Mexico. The first thing they will do is ask for your identification—give them the fake one I gave each of you. They'll ask you where you are from, so memorize your false Mexican identification— NOW. But if they don't ask you anything, you say *nothing*. But if they do, you say you're traveling to Guadalajara to visit family or to work so they don't suspect you're trying to cross the border. If you get nervous, they will ask you more questions…Where are you from? Where are you going? *Only* respond if they ask you. If not, you *keep quiet*. You have to act like you *don't* know the driver of the van you're in, because if you are standing too near to him or, if you are following him, they will suspect he is a coyote and will further investigate or detain you. *Do you all understand*?"

They all nodded, "Yes."

Most of the points on the fact sheet were about how to act like a Mexican, just in case. Something told Sofía this information would come in handy. It was overwhelming. This was the first time Sofía counted—*twenty people going on the trip*. She was so busy worrying that it would be the last time with her mother and her other sisters that she hadn't paid attention to the details of the people just yet. Little Carmelita was behaving nicely because she was still in an atmosphere where the movement of people and some surrounding faces were still normal. At last, the coyote shouted, "Grab your things. Everyone on the bus, *now*!"

As instructed, they mounted the bus, one you would typically find anywhere in Central America. Sofía struggled trying to focus on what was happening because she was still thinking about her mother. *I love my mother, my family, and my country. I miss her food already. Who will love me and take care of me like she does? I won't be there to take care of her. How can I ever say goodbye?* She reached down for her backpack and forced herself to say goodbye.

Betina wrapped her arms around her daughters and granddaughter. She held them tight, and reminded them to ask in faith for anything they needed. Her last words were, "I hope you girls arrive safely and that nothing bad happens to you. God will be there with you every step of the way." They hugged and turned toward the bus.

Sofía, Carmen, and Carmelita were the first to get on, so they took the first row. The twenty courageous travelers were tightly packed inside a vehicle meant for twelve to fifteen, depending on how the seats were arranged. Each had their own reason for leaving their country behind, but now they had a common sense of purpose to fulfill.

Chapter Five

The First leg and Already Sick

Q. How many miles is it from the Guatemala-Mexican border to the US-Mexican border?

A. 2,271 miles. It takes approximately 44 hours without stopping. That is a lot of travel for a baby.

All of a sudden, Carmelita began to cry. She sensed the unfamiliar discomfort her mom and Sofía felt, as they said goodbye to loved ones. There had been a lot of commotion the last few days. Things happened so fast, leaving Carmelita overwhelmed and confused. But onward they drove as evening time approached—about four hours without stopping. Nobody said a word. Everyone in the van seemed nervous; tension was high as they maintained their silence. Sofía spent the time crowded in her seat imagining different scenarios. No one could predict what they would encounter along the way.

At one point, the driver stopped to pick up another girl, about twenty-one-years-old, and a baby of about two or three years old. They squished in the seat next to Sofía and Carmen. That made twenty-two people plus the driver jammed in a van. Sofía let out a breath she didn't realize she had been holding in. She felt safer when that girl came aboard because now there were more women.

They began to talk cautiously. Jessica was from El Salvador. She too had decided to leave her country to escape domestic violence. Instantly they bonded. She and Carmen both had the task of caring for babies on this journey, so it was not long before they shared their dreams for a better life.

Sofía spoke softly but proudly, "I am going to help my sister with the baby. I could never be separated from them. We are going to live with our aunt in New York. We'll go to school there and get jobs to help pay for the cost." Jessica would be heading for California where her sister was going to receive them in the US.

Carmen was breast feeding the baby and took care of Carmelita's hunger. "Sofía, how are you doing? Are you hungry yet?" she asked.

Sofía replied, "No. I ate those tamales mom made for us about one hour before leaving. I'm not quite hungry yet. We need to save the snacks for as long as we can...remember what happened to our uncle."

Stillness surrounded the passengers. Within the stillness, at most, you could hear occasional soft whispers. The long drive, the quiet, and the heat were taking a toll on Carmelita. They were driving over desert-like terrain. Parts of the route were super-hot and other parts were very cold. Other than the one tiny baby blanket they packed, there were no other blankets or pillows for comfort. They continued to drive on for six more hours of silence. That brought them to the Mexican border. By that point, luck seemed to be with them, given that it was late night when they crossed into another country. They were fortunate they hadn't gotten stopped by any border patrols...so far.

Once in Mexico, they arrived at a farm-like Mexican ranch. It was two o'clock in the morning. The driver dropped them off and disappeared in a flash. Sofía watched him drive away. "Do you think he's headed back to Guatemala?"

"Probably," Carmen replied in a soft whisper. "Where else would he be headed?"

One by one the passengers were escorted into a large room on the side of the main farm house. As she entered, Sofía saw even more people there—about ten. She instantly felt relieved; at least there they encountered more women. Inside, each person found a spot on the floor to call their own and began to adjust to their new surroundings. There was only one bathroom for everyone. A small line formed ever so discreetly as they took turns using the restroom. Even then, silence prevailed.

"Sofía, you should eat now while everyone is getting settled. It will help you sleep better," advised Carmen.

Food was the last thing on Sofía's mind. She did not observe anyone eating or moving around much. But after much debate in her mind, she was able to take out a few crackers to nibble on. Without saying a word, she watched over the baby sleeping peacefully in her sister's arms. But neither Sofía nor Carmen were able to rest. They continued to share short, whisper-light conversations with their new acquaintance, Jessica. They were not sure who among them they could trust and didn't dare take the chance. Everyone kept their distance, but together, they all stayed quietly in their little spot on the hard floor until 6:00 AM.

Bright and early, a new driver appeared at the farm door. With a cattle whistle he motioned for them to go outside. He proceeded to separate the men from the women. Sofía gripped her sister's hand while Carmen held the baby close to her chest. He then guided all the women into one van, and all the men into another, which would follow it close behind during the next part of their journey. The windows were blackened so no one could see in.

They took off, continuing to head North for yet another eight hours. They stopped just twice for timed bathroom breaks. Nobody shared any food during the ride, as each person brought the estimated amounts needed to last for themselves as long as possible.

Sofía turned to Carmen and asked, "Why do think we never see the drivers eating, sleeping, or conversing with the travelers? It seems like they never stop watching us and our surroundings. Where do they go when they are not with us? Do you think they're making plans for us? When do they use the restroom?"

Carmen rolled her eyes and shrugged her shoulders. She didn't notice things like Sofía did—although they both agreed the rest-stops and houses seemed to be predetermined along the way. Jessica leaned over and whispered, "Throughout the route, there is a network of lodgings that become part of the plan. During my first time through someone told me the coyotes prearrange payment to the owners of these ranch houses to allow their passengers to stay the night, use their bathrooms, take showers, and fill up with gas. Some of them are church-related and some even offer basic food and snacks for sale. Everybody wants to earn a profit from us wherever they can. It's a business for sure."

During the daytime, the passengers could only leave the bus to use the bathroom, one at a time, so that no accidental neighbor, passerby, local police, or migrant official could notice the movement. Sofía learned how clever the coyotes were by prearranging every leg of the journey, with the stop times and bathroom breaks so precise that no one would conclude they were smuggling migrants.

Wondering still about the comings and goings of the driver, Sofía quietly asked, "Carmen, do you think our driver would ever take off without the passengers and leave us stranded here?" She was always thinking two steps ahead of Carmen, always thinking about the 'what ifs.'. Sofía also pondered why people follow the rules and why other people break them.

After discussing the experience so far, they figured this bus driver would never leave without them because of his leadership skills. Like rounding up a herd of cattle, he was constantly calculating and re-calculating, and never took his eyes off them as he repeated, "Hurry up!" "We don't have a lot of time!" and "Stay close!" He made sure each of his passengers was alert to the surroundings, acted appropriately, and stayed within his sight.

Carmen let out a snicker, "I imagine he needs to get his paycheck! Why else would anybody want to do this? It's just another job for him, I guess."

Just about then, the girls noticed that Carmelita wasn't acting right. She had come down with some kind of sickness. Her nose ran, she was sneezing, and though she had no fever, she coughed a lot. Her cries worsened as she wriggled around. Nothing seemed to make her comfortable. When she coughed, it seemed to hurt and she whined even more. They both hoped that perhaps it was a simple cold and nothing more serious. The baby's illness couldn't have come at a worse time.

Tapping her feet and stumbling her words, Carmen said, "Sofía, give the baby one of your crackers or something! Do you think her cries are very loud?"

Sofía shrugged her shoulders and avoided eye contact, realizing they hadn't brought any baby medicine. She didn't want to worry her sister anymore and said, "Give me my niece. I'll hold her for a while and see if she calms down some. Maybe she'll fall asleep on my shoulders."

By now her cries bothered everyone on the bus. Sofía knew what everyone on board was thinking. It was not typical to encounter a sick baby out and about—that would likely draw unwanted attention, something they desperately did not want. She looked up at Carmen, as they both tried to soothe her.

"Everyone is going to think we are a bunch of delinquents. No sick baby should be on this bus. I feel so badly for her. She should be home in bed, with mom," Sofía whispered.

The bus driver yelled out, "*Silence* the baby!"

Carmen and Sofía knew they had to keep little Carmelita silent and occupied. If anyone heard her at a routine stop or traffic light, the crying and coughing would raise suspicion, and they surely would be discovered. Every now and then the driver would glance in his rear-view mirror with a death stare, to remind Carmen that a loud crying baby is a red flag for anyone within earshot.

Around late afternoon they arrived at another ranch about five minutes from the nearest pueblo. The driver told them they would spend the night there. The driver always got off first. As the rest descended the vehicle, Sofía noted him talking to the owner and exchanging something he took out from his boot. Just as they were instructed, nobody else dared go near them. Single-file they entered another larger room. No sooner had they entered, the driver disappeared. *Where might this bus driver be headed in such a hurry? Whatever the reasons, I'm guessing things are on schedule, running smoothly like clock-work.*

"Carmen...Have you noticed that neither the drivers, the coyotes, or the ranch owners talk to any of us? They maintain their distance. They speak with so few words, some stern glances and some gestures...Why are their behaviors so unfriendly and mysterious? It makes me feel nervous watching them interact," Sofía whispered with a puzzled face.

Carmen replied, "No, and I don't care. It's just all part of the deal to get us where we need to go." Carmen knew it was best to be silent and not ask any more questions or wonder why. It was the only way to go forward.

Inside the room, to her delight, Sofía encountered more Hispanic females—two Ecuadorian women along with six men. Even though they were not from her own country, the sense of connection and identity as fellow migrants increased. Although still guarded, she and Carmen felt much safer in numbers, like a team of women who were now part of their group and spoke their language. They felt relieved even though there was limited camaraderie and chit-chatting at this stop.

Each migrant kept space between the other, no glancing, no sharing. The tension never died down. Sofía had always been scared from all the rumors about men assaulting women on these clandestine journeys. She remembered overhearing her older sisters and mom discussing this. Her heart raced. As she looked around the room, it was clear they had little to no protection. If something did happen, nobody would want to get involved. It was an awful feeling as those thoughts cycled through her mind.

At one point, the lady of the ranch entered the large room, and addressed the passengers with a brief, monotone voice, as if she had done this many times before.

"If you wanted to go outside of the room to get some fresh air, you can," pointing to the door and the one bathroom.

"You can buy food if you're interested." She offered cooked eggs to anyone who wanted to purchase food. "The water is free. There are small bags of chips and snacks for sale out front."

It was almost like a small deli where people could buy food on the go. Sofía and Carmen noticed her children playing around the side of the ranch when they drove in, but they were too afraid to walk around and explore. Nobody strayed off too far.

Carmelita's health had worsened. She was really sick. She continued to cough. Everyone could hear how much it hurt her as each strenuous breath out caused a whimper of pain.

In a desperate tone, Carmen asked Sofía, "What are we going *to do*? We don't have *anything* to give her to feel better or to *quiet* her cough!"

Before Sofía could respond, one of the older men appeared bothered and approached them. He offered Carmelita a candy lollipop. She clutched it in her little hands, but Carmen wouldn't let her eat it because they were too afraid of a man standing in their space. Instantly, she snatched it out of Carmelita's hand, which made her cry more.

The others grumbled and criticized the baby for the noise. They complained that immigration police would hear her and find them. "SHUT THAT BABY UP!" They were hostile, almost like an angry mob wanting the baby to stop. Sofía and Carmen were beside themselves, anxious and worried about what to do.

Sofía looked around and counted. There were a total of about fifteen people at this ranch who were up for the next leg of the journey. They stood attentively waiting to hear instructions. The lady returned after about twenty minutes. "You can take a shower." With more emphasis than before, "Do NOT use much water and NO more than five minutes! If you do, I will *charge more*! Women go first." There were about nine or ten men and they would go after.

There was an energetic vibe of gratitude in the air, that after several days now, they could refresh themselves with water. The girls hoped that a shower would help the baby. The line of migrants scurried over to the four, outdoor make-shift shower cabins. There were a few gasps...the water was very cold.

After their quick shower they noticed Carmelita was running a fever. She coughed a lot more, with more wheezing. The same older man who had offered her the candy lollipop before also noticed that she was getting worse. Once again, he got close to them and handed her a cough drop with an adult-strength Tylenol capsule. Carmen panicked that her baby was too young and the medicine might harm her. With a kind smile she accepted it then turned and slid it into her pocket. She didn't dare give it to Carmelita out of fear.

Under pressure, Carmen became resourceful. Trying hard not to panic, she took out the hidden cell phone buried deep in her clothing, and called their mother. As if she were performing an operation, she pressed each number on the keypad and cleared her throat, "Mom, it's me. We are OK. We are on a ranch somewhere in Mexico. Everything has gone well so far, but the baby has become sick with a fever, runny nose, and awful cough.

What should I do??" She described in a very low voice how angry the other passengers were.

Betina cried, which made Carmen cry, which made Sofía cry too.

Carmen, still panicking, repeated in slow motion, "We don't know what to do!"

The other siblings and Betina were all huddled around the phone listening to Carmen. Their older sister Alma, the nurse, took the phone and said, "Give just half the dose of Tylenol that the man has given you. Split the pill and be very careful because Carmelita is still just an infant. You were right to be worried. But it will be OK. Just give her half the dose. We love you!"

When they hung up, Carmen did as Alma had instructed. Then she took out a piece of clothing from her bag, wet it, and put it on the baby's head to keep her cool. Sofía held little Carmelita in her arms for hours until she finally fell asleep. During the night, her fever subsided. Gazing at her sleeping niece, she prayed. *Please Lord, make this illness go soon, and please don't allow Carmen or I to become sick. Thank you.*

It had been three days and nights since they left their home or slept in their own bed. Three days on the road with strangers. Carmen and Sofía may have dozed off a bit here and there, but they got through the night between vigilance of their surroundings, worry from the unknown, and pure exhaustion. Carmelita slept all night.

Chapter Six

Squished In

Q. How many people fit in an extended cab pickup truck?

A. Legally, five.

On the fourth day away from home, traveling with strangers who all wanted the same thing, Carmen and Sofía were exhausted. Thankfully, Carmelita seemed to be doing better. They hung around that morning on stand-by, idly waiting for an indication of where they would be heading next. There weren't many exchanges of conversation among the group, and the air was filled with apprehension. Sofía's eyes often wandered around with silent worry, but she stayed close to her sister. They had nothing to do but wait.

As that Wednesday morning turned into the afternoon, the girls confessed to each other about how they were feeling. "I'm a little anxious without our home surroundings, without mom, and without mom's breakfast. I can almost smell the kitchen aroma when she cooks. I miss seeing her." Sofía was more fearful about leaving her mom and sisters behind, and what awful things might happen to them on the journey, while Carmen felt relieved of the violence she escaped, and the future freedom she would find in the US. Her thoughts of what they were doing and where they were going started to sink in, as she tried to refocus on the paradise they were promised.

Carmen replied, "The only thing I can think about is my ability to go forth in a new country with my baby. I keep thinking about what Gunner will do if he finds us, and how I am going to provide for her alone in the US with no job and no permanent residency—*yet*. But I am so relieved to leave the last two years of my life back in Guatemala." Carmen was determined to plow through any obstacle and find a way to meet her new life-goals.

With nothing to do, they decided to buy the eggs from the women at the ranch. They were quite cold, very greasy, and partially raw. "Disgusting," Sofía said out loud. "It looks like mush." But she ate them anyway, with a few of the crackers they had stashed away.

"I'm just thirsty." Carmen wasn't hungry. She was very frail. With all the worry from her daughter's illness and thoughts about the life of abuse she was running from, she had no appetite. She hoped she could make enough breast milk to nourish her baby and to help her recover from whatever virus she came down with.

"What do you think Gunner will say when he finds out she is gone?" She paused. "Will he go after her in the US?" She paused again. "Could he find us?" So many thoughts Carmen shared with Sofía. Breastfeeding her daughter comforted her, knowing that little Carmelita would be safe from a violent upbringing. She was sure that her daughter would have a better future ahead of her, very far from her father. "I'm so very glad and thankful I have you by my side."

Sitting on the floor, Sofía had a moment to reflect some more on what *she* had left behind. *I'm accompanying Carmen at our mother's request... I love my sister dearly and only want the best for her and my niece, but I'm terrified of my own uncertain future, and what might lie ahead for me.* She stared off, hoping her sister wouldn't see her worried face. "*At the same time, I feel I needed to complete my duty for the welfare of our whole family....but with so many obstacles yet to encounter, so much could go wrong.*" So many mixed emotions ruminating in her head and in her heart. *Even if I do make it, what will I do? How will I do it? I don't know any English, I have no money, I haven't finished my schooling, and I'm going to live with my mom's sister who nobody has seen in over twenty years, I think.* It was a lot for a teen to contemplate.

Jessica, Sofía, and Carmen were situated in one corner and the men in another. Sofía continued to look around, always with vigilance. The men were of all types. Some older, some married, some young, some single. She would unassumingly eavesdrop on their conversations every now and then, without getting too close to their space. Listening intently to the men's dialects—Guatemalan, Honduran, Salvadoran, and Nicaraguan—she could discern from which Central American country they each came. That was kind of amusing to her.

No question, the girls still felt scared to be around the men. Many of the men were returning for another attempt and crossing the border, and hiding from border patrol who had detained them once—or twice already. *I wonder what atrocities they might be fleeing from? Do they have wives and children they're leaving behind? Do they miss their families as much as I do? Do they have a place to go or have sponsors waiting for them? Surely they have to have some reason to be here. What obstacles...or worse...what dangers might they have experienced getting to this point? Are these men as scared and afraid like I am?*

Suddenly, exactly at 2:00 PM, a new bus driver appeared, this time with a different kind of transportation. It was an extended cab pickup truck with double doors on each side. Sofía noticed that it also had very dark tinted windows so no passersby could see in. It had two rows of seats to accommodate two people up front and three in the back—under normal circumstances. This cab was not the model that had back doors which opened to access the cargo of people they would be carrying behind. She was curious to see how all of these travelers would fit into it.

The coyote got out, approached his new passengers, and told them exactly how they would get in. First, the two Ecuadorian women, one with a two-year-old baby on her lap. Next, Carmen holding Carmelita on her lap, then Sofía, and, lastly, Jessica with Jessica's baby. He motioned for them to get into the back seat. All the females with their babies lifted themselves up inside the truck. That was a total of seven squished in tight. Then he told the men to get in the back, one by one, and lay down on the cargo floor of the extended cab. They each had to lay down in such a way, first horizontal, the next vertical, the next horizontal, then vertical, etc., until the bottom of the cab space was full to capacity. That made a total of eight men, lying down.

They could not move around, get up, or even scratch an itch. After the men settled in the cab—on their backs, the driver covered them up with a tarp. Successfully disguised, the truck appeared as though it was carrying what cargo trucks typically do. Sofía shuttered as she peered back at them. *This truck has human beings lying down, covered up, barely able to breathe, in hopes of getting to a place that will allow them to have a better life than the one they left behind. God bless them.*

It was very hard for her to comprehend that underneath that tarp there were at least eight men risking their lives on a mission for hopefully, a better future. As a rule, they were ordered not to talk to each other. The vision of each one getting in and arranging their body in the cab floor haunted her, and made her more anxious about what was to come. *I hope these men follow the rules.*

Chapter Seven

Retenes, Hongos and Desert Animals, Oh My!

Q. What's *more* frightening: Secretly hiding from the police, being assaulted by a cartel gang member, being bitten by a rattlesnake, scorpion, black widow, or Gila monster, or unexpectedly fainting?

A. Anything that causes you to lose control is frightening: Authority intimidates with power, gangs use violence, reptiles hiss, and fainting causes a sudden loss of consciousness.

Jessica began a conversation with Sofía and Carmen to pass the time. Coming from Central America also, she wanted to share the rumors she had heard about the dangers of the journey through Mexico, and she wanted to learn about what they knew—sort of girl talk and comparing notes. Very quietly she asked, "Besides the obvious hardship of leaving home, do either of you know anything about Los Hongos? Do you know what they look like? I *think* they could be spotted apart from other men, maybe would they be wearing the colors of Mexico: red, green, and white, and probably have lots of tattoos?"

Carmen replied, "Nah, it wouldn't be that obvious I don't think. Lots of people have tattoos. We have a family member who made it through to the border. He warned us of the drug cartels and organized crime that carefully watch for travelers along this very route. He said Los Hongos are corrupt vigilantes who take it upon themselves to track down fleeing migrants like us. We are their target. They could rape us, kill us, kidnap our babies, and take our possessions—our money, food, and phones—everything. Ironically, they are more dangerous to us than the Mexican Police or the Retenes because they will do anything to get rich, control people, and gain territory."

Sofía chimed in, "Wait a minute. Who are the 'Retenes'?"

Jessica responded, "The Retenes are different from the vigilantes or the Mexican Police. They are migrant officials. The Retenes are hired by the Mexican government to keep migrants and refugees—us— *out* of Mexico. They don't want us cutting through their country to get to the US. Their only job is to send us back immediately if we get caught. The problem that scares most travelers is that the Retenes aren't looking for ways to stop the Hongos. Because there are so few Retenes, little can be done to support migrants who are detained, except to send them right back to their country. It's the Hongos we really have to watch out for."

Carmen added, "I know from Gunner that over the years, Los Hongos, among other local corrupt groups, have spread throughout the routes the migrants travel on. It is very lucrative for them. They are more powerful than either the Mexican Police or the Retenes because they can do whatever they want, and in most cases, never be prosecuted. We just have to keep watching out for men who seem interested in us and get into our space. We should not engage in conversations with anyone."

Jessica's voice grew tense as she spoke to the girls, "Yes, we need to prepare for anything. These guys can be violent. They are known to kill anyone who is not from their country for whatever profit or reason. They will heartlessly rob migrants of their money and belongings, assault women, decapitate, assassinate, and just abandon them in the desert or leave them for dead. Vulnerable travelers *like us* make it easy for Los Hongos to even recruit people by forcing them to do their bidding and kill them if they don't. Do you remember when they massacred entire busloads—193 passengers? It was awful."

Carmen said, "My uncle explained to my mom that the Mexican Government doesn't have the people or money to stop migrants from coming, or investigating crimes by vigilantes and cartels who interfere in a migrant's journey. The bottom line is, the Mexican Government doesn't have enough resources to stop the corruption and assaults. As a result, Mexican citizens won't get involved in situations they can't do much about. It is unfortunate that most citizens who might witness a crime play it safe and turn their backs on the vulnerable, like us, who, through necessity, *have* to travel through Mexico en route to the US border. This I know for sure. It takes some brave people to dare cross through a country that does not want them."

Listening intently, Sofía spoke up, "These terrible stories scare me. They sound all too common." Inquisitively she asked, "Do you think anything will happen to us? What would they want with young girls and babies? We don't have any money. Are you guys scared? If we were to get caught and had no money for ransom, or refused to work for a cartel, would we be murdered just like that?"

Jessica saw the fear in her eyes. She tried to cheer her up, "Don't worry Sofía. Let's just stick together. It's true, there are probably hundreds or thousands of tales of injustices, but those who do manage to survive the fear will ultimately find themselves with a new and better life. I think we're going to be fine if we watch out for each other. Just keep thinking about it as an obstacle you will get over— like the wall we have to go over—and think about all the good that is going to be on the other side of the border. The US is going to be a safe haven for us once we get through Mexico. Everyone says we'll be happy there. We are going to make it, I'm sure."

Sofía thought about it and said to Carmen, "Well, Mom must have weighed all of this and decided that even you, her own daughter who is running from Gunner's injustices and the hardships his mother created for you and Carmelita, should still take the risk. Despite all the danger, the challenges would be short-lived as opposed to the lifelong possibility of a great future...making it well worth the trip, I suppose."

Carmen agreed, "Yeah, Even though this terrifies all of us, and we could possibly find ourselves in a bad situation with no recourse, no support, no aid, no justice—or worse—the possibility of never seeing mom or our sisters again, we all agreed it was best to go ahead with the plan. So far, I'm glad we did."

It was a somber yet honest conversation for the girls to have, but somehow it fortified them, deepened their bond, and their motivation to stick together, to overcome whatever lie ahead.

Sofía refocused on each of the drivers, the coyotes, and ranchers they had met. *I must stay strong and remember how they work tightly together, synchronously, to arrange these journeys with a goal to get the passengers to their destination safely. For them, it's a job, a way to earn money like everyone else. They use cell phones and calculate changes in both routes and transportation to facilitate their job and get us safely to the border. We'll get there.*

As if to convince herself, she took a deep breath and said to Carmen and Jessica, "Our guide communicates coyote to coyote, driver to driver, and ranch to ranch. They help each other like links in a chain of people—all connected from one end to the other. They seem too busy to want any harm to come to us—their clients. They seem like they want to get their job done right."

Jessica replied, "This is my third time doing this. I didn't get far the first two times. But I've learned that they act as look-outs for possible police or Retenes who might be ahead. If something they see looks suspicious as we pass by, the drivers will notify the next driver as well as the previous one. They would call each other immediately if they anticipate risks or any kind of setback, like a roadblock or an unusual movement—including suspect Hongos."

Carmen added, "Yeah, they continuously advise the passengers what we need to do if we get stopped or questioned. That is helpful and reassuring."

Sofía said, "The way the drivers appear and disappear so quickly, their behavior with us, and the interactions with the ranch owners makes me feel like the communication between these drivers is amazingly precise. They must be vigilant, skillful and smart, every step, every link of the way. I suppose they are risking *their* lives too."

A few hours into the next part of the route, one of the lead drivers from another van notified Sofía's driver that there was a Reten nearby in the direction they were heading. They wouldn't be able to pass without being stopped. He estimated a high probability they would be detained and warned him not to take any chances.

Sofía's driver turned their truck around without hesitation. He drove to a nearby spot off course, about ten minutes away. The spot was like a mini forest within the desert where his truck was partially hidden among the surrounding trees. They remained concealed in the truck for about thirty minutes. During that time, the driver allowed the eight men to remove the tarp and sit up in the truck. The women were told to stay put. Sofía couldn't help but notice the relief of the hot, sweaty men who could breathe again. *I feel so sorry they have to stay in that position for so long! I'm so grateful that although, even I too can barely move, at least I'm sitting up and can breathe the air.* Her opinion of some of the men seemed to be changing.

The driver received another warning from up ahead. He needed to drive them deeper into the desert near some even more dense trees, where the truck could now be completely hidden. Three minutes deeper in and Sofía could still hear the noises of cars going by. She knew they weren't too far off the main road. The driver allowed them all to get out and walk around. The women jumped out to un-squish and un-stick themselves. Sofía watched the men stretched their bodies every which way to feel alive again. But, as usual, the driver never stopped cautioning them to be quiet. "DO NOT wander off! Realize you can be discovered at any time!"

The constant threat of something happening affected Sofía given the previous conversation she had with Jessica and Carmen. The pressure was mounting. *I feel like I'm living somewhat of a nightmare and wish it would end soon. Already, I miss my mom, my siblings, my own bed and pillow, and what used to be. Nonetheless, I will hold onto the faith that everything will be worth it once we get to our aunt's house, just as everyone has promised it will be.*

It was now about 7:30 at night and very dark. The stars were out. Nighttime in the Chihuahuan Desert got very cold. Sofía remembered her teacher mentioning that the Chihuahua was the largest desert in North America, stretching from the Southwestern United States deep into the Central Mexican Highlands. She thought of her uncle and wondered, *How long will I be in this desert?*

Sitting out in the open, she filled her head with thoughts of the infamous black spider, La Viuda Negra, and the many scorpions she knew could be everywhere. There were so many in Mexico. There could have been bobcats, mountain lions, or jaguars that could lacerate a skull with a single bite. The coyotes were known to attack people. There were snakes with painful toxins like the Mexican black-headed snake or the rattlesnake. She thought, *What would happen if any of the passengers got bitten, and what would they do because they couldn't even get medicine to help a sick baby?*

Sofía whispered to Carmen, "Everyone knows the western diamondback is found in nearly every habitat of the Chihuahuan Desert, along with desert lizards—including the Gila monster, so the guides surely must be prepared to handle that, right?"

They both remembered studying about those things in science. Sofía knew creatures lived under rocks and only bit if they were approached. She adjusted position, making sure she did not sit near any rocks. *The rattlesnake*, she recalled, *comes out at night and would know where I'm sitting long before I even knew it was near me.* That frightened her. Anxious and afraid at what desert animals could be lurking, she wondered and quietly asked Carmen, "Do you think any of the other passengers afraid?"

Just then, something triggered baby Carmelita. She too was frightened. She had been sensing the tension from her mom and Sofía, and it scared her. She was in an unfamiliar place, and the people surrounding her had unfamiliar faces. There were all the noises from the night animals lurking nearby. It was dark and she was confused. Just then, she let out a loud cry as babies do when they are afraid. Sofía rushed to her side and immediately wondered if she had been bitten.

In an instant, the men got angry again. They weren't interested if she were bitten; they just wanted silence while they were hiding. They knew they would be caught if someone heard a baby crying out there in an odd location. They circled around the girls and demanded angrily, "*Shut that baby up*! If we get caught it will be her fault!"

Carmen began to feel dizzy. The trip had taken its toll on her fragile body. She was already so slim and hadn't eaten. She was overwhelmed by the nerves and worry from the trip, the heat, then the cold, her sick baby, and now all the men screaming at her. She tried her best to breastfeed the baby to calm her down but felt weak and nauseous.

Without warning, she passed out. She fell forward with the baby at her breast. Luckily, Sofía was standing right next to her. She didn't know what had happened to her sister but stopped thinking about all the dangerous creatures of the night and reached out. Sofía caught her sister and the baby in her arms as Carmen fainted right on top of her.

Two minutes later, Carmen opened her eyes and moaned. Sofía realized how tiny her sister was. Her body was cold and clammy. She hadn't eaten much in a long time. She didn't know how she was able to produce enough milk for the baby. Sofía's worries multiplied. First Carmelita, and now Carmen. She held them tight and wondered, *How will we ever make it to the US?*

The same man who had given baby Carmelita a sweet candy lollipop earlier walked over and offered Carmen one. This man's face showed compassion for the young Carmen and her baby, as he fanned her with his jacket. By then, the gesture allowed them to trust him a bit, even though they had earlier discussed they would trust no one. He had been kind and generous with his candy and Tylenol. It was comforting for Sofía to trust someone else on this trip—a man who could perhaps protect them the rest of the way. After that last gesture of kindness, both she and Carmen let their guard down...just a little.

All the girls seemed to stick near this man as he chatted with them. He said, "That baby Carmelita reminds me of my own granddaughter." He told the story of how his own daughter and granddaughter were able to cross the border a few years ago. "She fled from the gang violence that was going on in my hometown in El Salvador. They've made a life for themselves in California. I hope to spend the rest of my days there with them, especially now that I'm older." He acknowledged the value of being near family, which touched Sofía's heart.

They waited about one hour off the main roads before moving on. By then, the guide received the next phone call... the coast was clear. *How many other times did the driver use this same spot for protection from the passersby...or was it just luck we were able to successfully hide here?* They wasted no time getting the men back in position, driving out from the trees, and getting back on the main road.

Relief filled the air. Surprisingly, Sofía found herself excited to get back into the truck. They drove about three more hours free and clear, with no sign of the Retenes or Hongos. She was sure they would have been stopped if they had gone on earlier.

But for now, the coast was clear and nobody got bit.

Chapter Eight

A Dropped Call

Q. If your cell phone suddenly gets disconnected, what do you assume happened?

A. It depends on what your conversation is about.

It was now late at night. The extended cab came to a stop at another ranch-like house. Everyone was directed to go into a large room off the side of the main entrance. The driver explained they were to sleep there until early morning, when they would depart on the longest and hardest part of the journey. As a matter of routine now, nobody was surprised there were no mattresses, pillows, or blankets.

Sofía could see peace of mind on the travelers' faces as she looked around. The emotions were running steady as they contemplated being able to sleep safely for a while. She could tell they all understood; even though they found themselves in a desert at night far from their homes, for now, they were safe from Retenes and being sent back home. Until further notice, they would be protected from danger and from Los Hongos, at least for a little while.

"How nice a change in space for the men who were situated all that time under the tarp in the back of a truck. At least they can stretch out on this ranch floor," Sofía said to Carmen.

"I know. It had to be brutal for them. But let's take the spot in the corner over there, away from the entrance. I don't want to be near any of the men." She set down her bag to mark their territory in the room. They had only the chamarras, a sweatshirt-like jacket, they brought. "I'm so glad we have the baby blanket; it isn't much, but it is a comfort to Carmelita."

Once everyone settled on their spot in the designated ranch room, Sofía and Carmen were anxious to contact their mother and let her know how they were doing. They were not moving in a truck or in any immediate tricky situation; they could finally make a phone call home and connect with their mother. Jessica, her baby boy, and the Ecuadorian ladies stayed close by. They quickly became safety zones for each other.

Long-distance cell phone calls were expensive, and they were grateful they had added prepaid minutes before they left. They decided it would be prudent to first call their Aunt Martina in New York to let her know what was happening. It was an awkward call because they had never spoken to her before this—only their mother had on rare occasions. They spoke just long enough to let her know the number of days into their journey and their best guess at what their arrival date would be at the border. The rest of the conversation was dominated by their aunt warning them...

"Do *not* to talk to immigration or tell them any details, including those of baby Carmelita! Can you imagine? I fear what might happen when Gunner finds out!" Aunt Martina did not sound pleased at all. "Let me remind you that Amber Alerts exist in Guatemala, and that Gunner would not be afraid to accuse Carmen of kidnapping." Her tone was clear—she did *not* want to be any part of that.

The voices of the travelers got louder as they became more relaxed. The others in the group must have also realized at this moment on the journey that it was the perfect time to contact families back home. Many conversations could be heard all across the room. Sofía listened. Just as she and Carmen took advantage of the stop to call home, the others did too. She observed they all seemed to be excited and hopeful talking to their loved ones. There was a special vibe in the air: they were all in it together, strangers or not. Together, they were not afraid.

The girls couldn't wait to call their mother. In very low voices, they took turns explaining to Betina all they had experienced so far. Their older siblings, who happened to be there, gathered around the phone just to hear them.

"How are you! How's the baby? I miss you girls terribly!" Betina was so excited to get the call. She tried to sound like she wasn't worried as she held back her tears.

Carmen replied, "Nothing has happened to us and Carmelita is so much better! We were able to buy eggs to eat. We came close to getting stopped."

Sofía blurted out, "Carmen fainted, but I caught her! A nice older man gave us candy." She was so happy to talk to her mom and sisters.

Although not thrilled that the baby had been sick, and then almost got pulled over, Betina responded, "I'm so glad you girls are safe and doing well. What part of Mexico are you in now?"

Carmen said, "We have no idea where we're located. We've just arrived at a ranch and everybody is calling home. We'll be here tonight. We met a few women who also have babies, so we stick together. Thank goodness Sofía is with me. I couldn't have done this without her."

Betina let them know, "Gunner hasn't come by as frequently as before, so, I know he's up to something. We are not sure, but he can't get to you or the baby now. Our lips are sealed. I'm so glad you are halfway there! And tell me, who is this older gentleman who was kind enough to share his candy?"

The time flew by, yet they spoke for almost an hour. Then, suddenly, they heard a *click* and the phone went dead. Sofía's mouth dropped open with panic, " We've been disconnected!

We're out of minutes already! There is so much more to say! Mom isn't going to know *why* we were disconnected*!* She'll never assume that we only just ran out of cell minutes…she'll think the worst!"

Panicked, Carmen squealed, "I didn't even notice the minutes were running low! We didn't have time to explain! We didn't know! Knowing mom, yes! She's going to fear the worst given how she worries about us. Now what are we going to do?"

Sofía agreed that their mom would agonize needlessly that something bad happened to them because they were cut off so abruptly. She and Carmen began to strategize where and how they might be able to buy more minutes.

Sofía shook her head and said, "By luck, we called our aunt before the minutes ran out, so at least Aunt Martina will be reassured we're coming." "That was the right thing to do."

Even though they were disconnected, the girls felt some relief that they could get in touch with their family back home. It was a good feeling to hear their voices. Carmen and Sofía knew in their hearts that neither of them could have made this journey by themselves. Growing more confident, Sofía laid down and closed her eyes, truly believing things would be fine for the first time since her journey began.

They snuggled up close to each other. It was obvious Carmelita had become more alert to all that was going on around her. She looked about at all the people surrounding her on the floor and remembered this was not her old bedtime routine. She clutched onto her tiny blanket which helped relax her, until she, too, began to sleep peacefully. Every now and then, she would let out a slight coughing noise. Some men would jump up or flinch their arms and legs as if they were ready to run when they heard her cough. But just as fast, they settled back down in their designated spot in the farmhouse. Finally, they were able to rest.

In the morning, it didn't take long for Sofía to notice the latest 'guide', 'coyote', 'driver', 'whoever' he was, as being very different from the others. He was much less agitated than the driver who dropped them off the night before. She observed his mannerisms. She told Carmen, "There is something different about this guide. You can tell by the way he handles the conversations with us. He speaks the Word of God. I have a good feeling about him. I'm convinced the Good Lord has sent him to guide us safely to our destination. I hope he is the *last* coyote we ever have to meet."

Carmen chuckled, "Yeah, He sounds like he's of the Christian faith. And you know, to be a Christian means that you share the same faith as the apostles, so he probably knows our patron saint of Guatemala, Saint James." She added, "There are a few stories of different religious coyotes who are good people, compassionate and humane, wanting to help those in need. Maybe we got lucky and he is one of them."

His name was Miguel. He was young, friendly, and offered kindness in the way he presented himself to the group. He commanded their attention with gentleness. When Sofía thought about the other coyotes, she noted that this was the first time one interacted with the passengers or hung out in the same room with their 'cargo.' The other ones kept to themselves. They disappeared in a heartbeat and shared very little conversation. Those men offered only what they needed to. This perception of Miguel brought peace of mind to her.

The señora of the ranch entered the room and gave them all free food: eggs, beans—better known as frijoles, and tortillas. This time, everything was cooked thoroughly and smelled delicious, just like home. The lady wasn't trying to become friendly with the travelers. She was indifferent once she delivered the food. And although she didn't shout at them in a demeaning manner like other stops, she put the food down and said to everyone in a casual manor, "Here's your food; over there you can take a shower, and over there beyond that building, you can walk around, but don't stray." That was it. Then she disappeared.

Sofía compared the ranches. *Why do some ranchers prepare lousy food and offer meager services at an additional cost, yet others, like this lady, give things to us for free? This time the food came almost with a touch of kindness. Things are looking up,* she thought as she smiled.

After eating, the girls were eager to line up to take showers. They were encouraged to go first because of the baby...another rule that became apparent. There were four outdoor showers all in a row. And cold, cold water again. But they knew that cold water was better than no water. Sofía had to convince herself that the water on this ranch would invigorate them enough to keep going. She prayed in the shower, and spoke to each of her body's cells, organs, and muscles. *Please accept this cold water so that I might stay healthy and fit for the journey because my sister and niece need me, and my mother depends on me.*

When she was done, it was Carmen's and Carmelita's turn. Sofía stayed vigilant outside the shower door so no men got near them, and Carmen could safely shower the baby. "Gosh, I hope this chilling water won't worsen her cough." Little Carmelita was not very tolerant of the cold water, but somehow, she understood that freshening up would happen quickly and there would be calmness afterwards.

On this ranch, they would spend the entire day and probably well into the night. They never knew when they would get their next instruction, only that it could come at any time. So they needed to be ready and alert, waiting to depart at a moment's notice.

As Sofía watched and pondered the activities of the others, she couldn't help but notice the kindness floating about. The Ecuadorian girls, Sheila and Abrielle joked, laughed, and slept near them. They had absolutely nothing to do. She turned to Carmen and said, "There's definitely something different about this stop. It seems like it has good-hearted people working on it, because things are going really well. People are smiling. Maybe it's because we're getting closer?"

Carmen noticed it too, "This time, the people here seem more human, more compassionate with everything they're doing for the travelers. And that feels really good."

Behind the main building, Sofía also noted something different on this ranch. There were lots of cows roaming the land. "Carmen, isn't it ironic the animals are free to do the opposite of the migrants?" She pointed over to the other side where there was an interesting garden. The dry heat and full-on sun produced dozens of minuscule cactus flowers, sage, yucca, and willow, which was an all-encompassing view for them. "The sun and the moon shine equally on everyone, no matter where they are or who they are."

Carmen remarked, "I like this place. To have such a garden, there must be caring people with hearts living here. Maybe we'll grow a garden like this when we get to the US. Do you think our aunt has one?"

Sofía shrugged her shoulders. She was thinking about her days back at school. She thought about the geography she learned back home. "Much of the landscape surrounding this ranch has probably been formed through the volcanic intrusion from the neighboring mountains—very different than the landscape we were used to in San Marcos."

She imagined the magma pushing up and under the existing layers, creating mounds that would later erode into magnificent formations. "This is what allows this incredible floral and agriculture to grow here. Quite interesting. I wonder what the landscape will look like where we're going. Will there be any volcanic mountains there? Hopefully, this isn't the calm before the storm."

Proud of herself for remembering geography facts, she recognized the desert marigolds and barrel cacti, snake-weed, and Mexican poppy flowers from the pictures in her science class textbook. Her fear of desert animals, like at the last place, seemed to have subsided with the tranquility she felt here. Sofía considered herself intelligent and observant. She cared about her education and her surroundings. She didn't fit the stereotyped teen as ignorant or neglectful of learning. But soon, her thoughts brought her back to the current situation at the ranch. She needed to follow the rules and stay alert. *There will be plenty of time to dream later on, once we get to our aunt's house. I will learn English and lots more geography facts there!*

The girls played catch with a small rock they found on the ground near the garden. They continued to keep their distance from the others while Carmelita played with Jessica's little boy, three-year-old Gabriel. They say kids are resilient, and Carmelita was feeling more at ease. She had nursed and played—almost like her old self again. Carmen worried the diapers were irritating Carmelita's bottom, and if they did not get some soothing lotion for her soon, she would have something else to cry about.

Sofía noticed how much thinner her sister got in just a few days. *I hope my sister will stay strong enough to keep herself healthy and the baby satisfied the rest of the time on the road.* Although the day's temperature became oppressive and hot, their time outside in the daylight refreshed and soothed their worries. They could move about and enjoy the surrounding nature, now that half their journey was complete.

Inevitably, Gabriel caught Carmelita's cold. It was Gabriel's turn to come down with a fever and a terrible, relentless cough. The good news was, he was less of a crier and did not disturb the men as much as Carmelita did. And because the others did not want to catch the virus, they happily kept their distance.

Chapter Nine

The Final Send Off

Q. What is the pun in the meaning of the Guatemalan proverb, "Salir de Guatemala y entrar en guatepeor" ("Out of the frying pan and into the fire?")

A. The proverb is literally saying things are going from bad to worse. The pun part comes from the name Guate*mala*, where *mala* means bad, and guate*peor*, where *peor* means worse.

As the day rolled on, they continued to feel semi-normal and relaxed. Somehow or another, there was a lot less tension among the travelers. People moved closer into each other's space, sharing glances more often, even a smile or two. Everyone at least had the appearance of feeling safe and at ease that day.

Their latest guide Miguel spent the day hanging around them. He was Mexican. Sofía wondered, *Why would he want to help others pass safely through his own country? Compared to the other coyotes, he is an unusual guide. He probably gets paid a lot to do this. But...It doesn't seem like he's in it for the money.*

One by one, casually and without hurry, Miguel went around to each of the travelers and asked how they were and how they felt about the journey. There was even some laughter now amidst the small talk. She remarked to Carmen, "This was the first time I've heard a laugh out loud in a week." Apprehension about the time that lay ahead had decreased, with the calm Miguel seemed to spread amongst the travelers. As the girls watched him move about, it didn't take long to trust that he didn't have an ulterior motive. On the contrary, he genuinely seemed like he wanted to get to know each one. He had been the only one who gave them real hope for the future.

At 6:00 PM, he called the group together. Sofía and Carmen had just returned from the bathrooms and left their bags neatly on the floor. With anticipation of somehow buying more cell minutes, Carmen remembered to plug in her phone to charge. She wanted it ready to go as soon as they had an opportunity. They left their carved-out spot, ran outside with the rest of the group, and stood confident next to the other women—Jessica, Sheila, and Abrielle.

Like a pastor speaking to his congregation, Miguel wished them, "Buena suerte. Les deseo a todos la buena suerte del mundo. Espero que llegues donde quieres estar, que todo salga bien, y que no te olvides de tu familia en casa si consigues salir adelante."

"Good luck. I hope that you get where you want to be, and all goes well, and that you don't forget your family back home if you make it through." He proceeded to give them the Word of God as he pulled out his soft-covered Bible. With his mild manner and without haste, he read several passages. Sofía and Carmen stood leaning against each other while others sat before him on the ground. Little Carmelita rested on Carmen's hip.

Carmen commented, "This coyote must feel it is his mission to minister to our group. He's empathetic and tries to ease everyone's worried mind. It seems like he wants to get to know us as humans, not as illegals or undocumented migrants."

Sofía agreed, "Yes! I like that it feels as if God Himself has ordained him to remind us we have hope for a better life where we are headed in North America."

Abrielle turned to them and nodded, "He's describing a preconceived idea about the evil that so many think we are committing, when we are only trying to escape our hellish life in our birth country. He recognizes we need a fresh start, or a new beginning that is safe from the actual evils we've experienced."

Sofía kept her opinion to herself. *That is true. Maybe he has experienced violence in his lifetime too. But there is probably a better way—or a right way—to do things. Regardless, this journey is what my mom, my sisters, and Carmen want, so I'm good with that.*

Through what turned into a sermon to the people, Sofía realized that the group was soon to be split up. She presumed the reasoning behind the split was that perhaps some had paid more than others. Miguel outlined the next leg of the journey for each of their separate destinations. Some of them would depart on foot through the desert, and others would go the main route on a tourist-type bus to reach the border. She grinned at Carmen and said, "Either way, no more vans or trucks. We are going to take the three-day ride on a bus!"

"The bus," Miguel explained, "will be the size of an average tourist bus known in North America as a Greyhound. It will have a bathroom on board for your convenience. Understand that the kind and size of tourist bus you're going to catch is dedicated exclusively to Mexican tourists—people who like to travel within Mexican borders. That is good for you because the probability of getting caught goes way down."

"Carmen, do you think the 'tourist' bus drivers are in on the trafficking? Would the coyotes pay the bus drivers to remain quiet? How enormous it will be! I wonder how many real tourists will fill it!"

Carmen smiled, "I was thinking the same thing. Wow. This is going to be roomy."

Jessica added, "The reason they need to use a big tourist bus is, if we go in any kind of car, and the coyote gets caught, it would mean many years in prison for him."

Miguel continued, "The bus that will pass by here in a few short hours routinely takes Mexican tourists from Mexico City to Guadalajara. It is also very near the border."

"For those taking the bus," he explained, "it is going to pass by along the highway at exactly 11:00 PM tonight. Be on guard...the ranch you are staying on is *exactly* three minutes from where it passes by—just long enough to pick up anyone standing there. There might be a disguised coyote on board. They rarely make themselves known unless something goes wrong. They avoid carrying identification and often use nicknames. If you are stopped, they will pretend to be a migrant like yourselves. Nevertheless, they are highly knowledgeable about border operations. They understand shift schedules and the stations of border agents. They understand how the aerial surveillance works, they are up-to-date on technologies used by border patrol, and they monitor everything that moves."

He exhorted, "*Be cautious like watch dogs*, pay attention, and don't stop monitoring for it to go by. It will go by *very* slowly, and you must flag it down, run, and catch it. If you miss the bus, unfortunately you will then be on your own. You will lose the chance to be guided further, and you will have to find your own way home!"

Hearing that, Sofía straightened up with her eyes wide open, "If that happens, we'll be lost for sure. Just like mom warned us."

He went on, "Those who catch it will get on and travel as a Mexican tourist until you reach Nogales. That's a three-day journey to get to the border. There you will get off." Sofía and Carmen looked at each other excitedly as they took in the information. They were eager to move on.

But then Miguel added the confusing part, "There is going to be a *yellow* taxi waiting about 20 yards away from where the bus will let you off in Nogales. *Don't* take the pink taxi or get into any white vans. The yellow taxi is going to be in front of a white house. The taxi is going to take you to a hotel."

The girls were overwhelmed. So many colors. Between the two of them, they hoped they would not mix them up. Sofía visualized the scene. She asked Carmen, "Can you imagine? And what if there was a white taxi with a yellow house or yellow taxi and a white hotel?"

"No! No!" "We can't let that happen. Stay focused," Carmen warned.

Sofía wasn't about to let any mix-ups happen. "We'll get it right," she assured her sister. "This seems easy enough. For sure, it won't be a great hotel, but I hope it will be an upgrade to the previous one-room ranch buildings where everyone scrambles for their own space on the floor. Maybe, there might even be pillows and blankets!"

Miguel relayed more instructions to the migrants. "Once at the hotel, the next coyote will be communicating to the main coyote, who will contact the person who holds the other half of your money. He is going to arrange the last of the payment."

"Let's hope a call from the him will alleviate any concern over our safety from the previous dropped call." The sisters agreed, "When the main coyote calls our mother for the rest of the money, mom will assume if we've made it that far, then we're doing OK. That's a relief!"

The words that came next from Miguel were critical. "These next items are going to determine if you make it or not." He warned, "Be very aware you will pass by many Retenes from this point on." Sofía started to sweat. She looked at Carmen and right back at Miguel. She didn't dare miss a word.

"When they stop you—and they will—they are going to ask many questions, like, 'Where are you going?' and 'Where are you coming from?' They'll ask you for your Mexican ID card, so *always* have it ready. *Memorize* your name and the information on it. *Know how* to pronounce every word correctly."

His delivery was serious and firm, especially when he emphasized the identification. He said with a steady, deep tone, "Make sure you have it. Everybody check for it right now! Make sure you keep it in an easily *accessible* place on your body. We don't want any mistakes."

He paused and demonstrated, "They'll look you firmly in the eyes. They are trained to make visual contact. They will look you up and down for the slightest nervous jerk or twitch, so stay calm!"

After another long pause, Miguel stated, "If you appear to be nervous, they will know immediately you are a migrant traveling through their country. They won't hesitate a second, and they won't waste their time asking any more questions to confirm if it's true or not. They will sweep you away to their headquarters and deport you within hours. They *don't* care about your issues or reasons for wanting to go to the US. Their job is to find you and send you packing. They just want you *out* of their country."

The travelers all gasped simultaneously. Nobody wanted to be sent back. Carmen mouthed the word, "Gunner," as she and Sofía glanced at each other and then down at Carmelita. They had come too far.

He gave his best tip, "They will try to trick you with semantics. They'll mix up words to see if they can catch you. For example, they'll ask, 'De qué estado vienes?' If the Retenes hear you responding with words from a dialect different from how they speak, you don't have a chance of making it through."

Sofía knew what he meant. This was covered with the first coyote. She felt a little confidence growing.

Miguel pleaded, "Everyone begin—if you haven't already—to memorize the details and to be cautious. You *need* practice speaking with a Mexican dialect, I can't emphasize that enough. And above all, practice remaining calm."

His instructions lasted about two hours. Sofía had already practiced these things a few times. She was impressed with Miguel's knowledge and his ability to express what needed to be said so that each traveler heard and understood. He was patient. No one asked him any questions. Sofía mumbled under her breath, *No one dares speak out loud for fear of acknowledging what we are actually doing.*

Carmen sighed, "I wish every coyote was as understanding and communicative as he is. He talks to us and looks at us like we're human. I think he really cares what happens to each of us. I think he wants us all to be successful, no matter what happens. He sees that some of us have babies. What do you suppose makes him different?"

Sofía processed everything they had experienced up until this point. She replied, "I don't know…Maybe because he read from the scriptures? What I want to know is, how many migrants do you think must have been successful traveling this same route before? How many other times did Miguel preach to migrants and refugees? It makes sense to me that each of the coyotes' behavior is reflected in all they must have seen and accomplished over time. I'm guessing we got lucky."

At 8:00 the instructions ended and the prayers began. Miguel made a point to circle around and pray for each of them. He prayed for those present, for those who had already made their destination in the United States, and for those who were yet to cross through. As Sofía looked around, she saw everyone crying or weeping softly. It turned into a very emotional event. One by one, Miguel prayed over them and gave each a special heart-felt hug.

Carmelita was holding steady on Carmen's lap. Miguel bent down and gave little Carmelita a hug too. There was some sunlight still left in the sky but Sofía knew it would not last long. She automatically became anxious as she glanced over in the distance, thinking, *Three minutes away.* As the darkness set in, she did not want to lose sight of that designated bus spot. It was beginning to get cold out. Carmelita started to whine in her soft, nagging baby voice. It was about her bedtime, and she snuggled up to Carmen while still on her lap, hoping to keep warm.

After the cautionary instructions, and the prayers, Miguel made his way around the group again, person by person, giving each one his individual attention. He understood that they all had their own circumstances and reasons for wanting to leave their country behind. He knew that many would not be familiar with what lies ahead once they get to their destination. He offered individual advice and tips, describing what they might be up against in the United States, once they did make it.

When he got around to Sofía and Carmen, he looked them both straight into their eyes. "What you're probably going to find at your aunt's house might not always be full of the opportunities you have been told. You need to be prepared mentally because life is going to be hard...It *might* even be worse."

What? Sofía was shocked! That was the first time she had ever heard any of this. She was stunned, *Worse?* Her mind was trying hard to make sense of what he said. She knew she would have some language barriers at first, but she never dreamed it could go from bad to worse. She ruminated, *Worse? How? Why?* That thought never occurred to her! When her mother asked her to leave her own country to accompany her sister and the baby—freedom from domestic violence to a better life—she knew it was risky, but she never once contemplated worse.

Miguel's words shook her. Her eyes widened. *Did everyone get the same message?* She felt a chill go down her spine. Up until that moment, she assumed what everyone also believed—that the United States was the land of wealth and opportunities. She was certain... had convinced herself that eventually they would be fine. Miguel's words left her dumbfounded. It had never crossed her mind that running away from a dangerous life might turn out more challenging than the one she and her sister left behind. *There must be some mistake.*

Chapter Ten

Plans Changed!

Q. How fast can you run in three minutes?

A. Whatever it takes...if you have to.

As Miguel continued sharing from his heart, praying, and advising the travelers with all he knew, it was already 10:00 PM. He needed precious time with each one and there were at least fifteen. Just then, his cell phone rang. With a worried look on his face, he excused himself over to a nearby cactus and took the call.

The plans had changed. He learned that the tourist bus was running ahead of schedule and would pass by the designated spot in *exactly* three minutes. In an instant, Miguel called out to the travelers, "You need to run straight away to the spot and catch the bus, like *now!*" He took a quick look around at the travelers and repeated his words—only this time with a deep and forceful shout, "You have *exactly three minutes* to catch the bus. Go *now* as fast as you can!"

Sofía and Carmen turned and ran as fast as they could back into the room to get their few belongings. Carmelita bopped along on Carmen's hip. She was in a daze. Everyone made a mad dash into the room, scrambling like crazy to get what they owned. Sofía calculated out loud as she ran, "Oh no! Three minutes is what it's going to take to get from this ranch to the bus stop, and it's already on its way!"

They rushed into the room and scooped up their possessions. Sofía quickly threw the small baby blanket over her shoulder, grabbed her bag, and sweatshirt. Miguel continued to shout at them from outside, "Hurry up! Hurry!" Carmen held Carmelita close to her chest.

Sofía yelled over to Carmen, "Don't forget Carmelita's tiny backpack and grab the pampers!"

There was no time to think. Sofía was more orderly and faster than Carmen. She was a bit light-headed and had difficulty maneuvering around with her baby as she tried to process what was happening. In a split second, Carmen, seeing that Sofía had gathered her things already, yelled back to Sofía, "Take the baby and go! You go with the baby!"

Without missing a beat, Sofía grabbed the baby from Carmen and headed out the door toward the bus stop. It was pitch black and hard to see, but somehow every cell in her body sensed it was just three minutes away...maybe two. In her mind, as if in slow motion, Sofía told herself, "Go slow, really, really slow." She needed to give her sister enough time to catch up. But her feet weren't listening. Sofía panicked as her emotions were getting the best of her... *What will I do with my sister's baby if I make the bus and Carmen is not behind me?*

Stumbling along, Sofía let out a wail and burst out crying. And when Sofía's tears started falling, Carmelita began crying too. Carmelita was startled and confused at why she was suddenly on her Aunt Sofía's hip. She did not like seeing her mom left behind. Sofía composed herself as best she could to not further scare her niece. She cried as silently as she could, not knowing if her sister would make it in time. She heard her mom saying to her, "Go! Go! Go!"

Everyone around her was stumbling and falling down because the path from the ranch up to the bus stop was covered with stones, cactus, and uneven terrain. The night was moonless and black. Sofía couldn't see if her sister was coming. There was no time to look back and check. Instead, she ran as fast as she could with Carmelita on her hip. *I hope she is behind me...Please, God,... let my sister make this bus with me,* she pleaded into the darkness.

When she got to the bus, she grabbed the door handle with one free arm and hoisted herself up to the first step, almost tripping as she clambered up. Her tears were hard to notice between the cold air, the running, and sweating. She tried hard to remain calm and casually walked down the aisle, to the back of the bus. When she and Carmelita collapsed into the seat, she closed her eyes tightly with fear and apprehension. She didn't want to see who else made it.

As she caught her breath, her eyes opened slowly. Only then did she realize that all the other people had indeed passed her in the race to catch the bus. Everyone...except her sister. Sofía looked around, counted, and saw that the others were already seated on the bus. Frantic, she stood up and looked out the nearest window and saw Carmen running as fast as she could. Sofía stood frozen in time. As if in slow motion, the driver moved his hand over the lever, a switch that applies pressure to the pistons that were about to close the door.

Carmen saw it too. She hustled even faster, grabbed the door pole, and swung herself on. Tiny, petite Carmen jumped so high and fast, she skipped two steps and knocked over the mini trash can next to the bus driver's seat, but...she made it.

They were the last ones on. All the other migrants had passed them in that miraculous three-minute sprint from the ranch. Sofía, who always kept a vigilant eye on who was traveling with them, kept counting the heads over and over. To her amazement, all the ones who were supposed to get on the bus made it.

Right away, Carmen spotted her daughter sitting in the very back of the bus with Sofía. As the pistons closed the doors, she dashed her way down the long aisle, making her way where, she too, collapsed into the seat and breathed heavily.

The bus had some light, but overall, it was dark inside. The sisters wasted no time getting comfortable in the back seats. Sofía liked the idea that their new home for the next few days would be on a large bus with a mixture of 'real' tourist travelers. She smiled of contentment and made peace with herself. *At least we won't go in and out of ranches anymore—at least I hope not.*

Still catching their breath, they looked at each other all at once and realized what had just happened, and what could have happened. They sat still and stared for a moment, then hugged. As hard as they tried, there was no holding back more tears in front of the baby. No words were needed. Their eyes said it all…They…almost…missed…the…bus! Sofía hugged her sister so tight as she replayed how close they came to missing the connection. But she refused to allow any thoughts of being separated creep in, ever again.

Suddenly, it occurred to Carmen to look for her cell phone. Sofía saw her reach for their bag, then scramble for Carmelita's bag, and then swipe down her pants pockets. Sofía knew what that meant. Carmen screamed under her breath, "I left the phone!"

Sofía remembered seeing her plug the phone into the wall for charging as they were getting their final send-off instructions from Miguel. "Oh my God! You left it charging!"

Even though Sofía had cautioned her, with the rush, she inadvertently left it behind. Neither could believe what bad luck that Carmen forgot to unplug it. Carmen could barely get the words out, "That phone was such an important part of our security! Now we have no way to communicate for the next three days!" This time, Carmen sobbed uncontrollably as Sofía consoled her.

They didn't dare talk very loud with all the bus passengers on board. Carmen motioned with her lips as if yelling, "Now what are we going to do? We don't know anyone here in Mexico! What if we get lost? What if something happens to us now? We don't have a way to communicate home!" And the tears kept rolling. "I keep rehearsing that three-minute dash scene in my mind! How did I forget the phone? I think it will be my fault if anything happens to us!" She looked at her baby, "How could I have done something so stupid? I cannot believe I've jeopardized our safety!"

Perhaps it was a lack of sleep, or too much worry, or not enough nutrition. All kinds of negative thoughts came tumbling out. They spoke to each other so lightly, hoping the other people could not hear them. But one of the Ecuadorian girls, Sheila, seated in the row ahead of them, did hear her. She turned around and whispered, "What happened?"

Sofía whispered back, "Carmen accidentally left the cell phone plugged into the wall."

Sheila smiled and told her, "Not to worry," as she pulled out her cell phone for them to borrow. Sofía felt so relieved she sank probably another foot into her seat.

Carmen reached for the phone, thought for a moment, scratched her head, then began dialing. Sofía had written her aunt's phone number in pen under her upper arm, but just then realized, she did not even know her own mother's phone number. "Carmen, It feels like a miracle that you know mom's number by heart. Thank Goodness! We're all so used to just hitting the send button each time." As Carmen dialed the number, Sophía thought, *The idea of going forward without a phone scares me, but I can't let Carmen feel any worse...How did we not anticipate losing the phone or the need to have more paid minutes? What else have we not anticipated?*

Now that they had the chance to call, they would do so right away before something else stopped them. They were desperate to assure Betina they were safe. They needed to let her know they did *not* have a phone with them now, and also that they just ran out of minutes when they had been abruptly disconnected the last time they spoke.

It was a lot to take in: the very long day with nothing to do, then a spiritual retreat with Miguel, the sudden rush onto the bus, and now, the phone. Sofía sensed that Carmen felt guilty at the thought of what they would have to do without a phone. It was stressing Carmen. Nevertheless, they took advantage of the opportunity to use Sheila's phone and as quietly as they could called their mom.

Betina wept with them and said, "Just buy another one!"

Sofía responded in frustration, "From where? How?"

The journey was taking its toll. Carmen snapped, "Mom, have you been listening? Has it sunken in yet, that two of your youngest daughters are traveling on a dangerous route through the worst section of Mexico to start a new life in a world far from yours?"

What was Betina thinking? Sofía thought to herself. *We can't just go stop and buy a phone. We are so fortunate to have made friends with Sheila and that she let us use her phone. Be brave,* she repeated to herself.

It wasn't long before Carmen and Sofía calmed down. Speaking with their mother gave them hope and relief. Carmelita quickly fell asleep on Carmen's lap. They drove uninterrupted all night long. Each time Sofía used the bathroom, she took advantage of a private moment and practiced her Mexican accent.

By around early morning, they passed the anticipated Reten station. The police lights flickered, and the sirens rang for them to stop. The bus was pulled over. Two Retenes mounted the bus and sharply demanded that everyone get off. They made everyone stand in a straight line. One of them pulled Sofía out of the lineup and began questioning her apart from the others.

"What's your name?"

Sofía gave her Mexican name, "Isabela."

"Who did you come with?"

"My sister."

"Let me see your identification."

"Which one is your sister?" Sofía knew to keep her mouth shut as much as possible and pointed over to Carmen.

That is when they began to question Sofía even further because, oddly enough, Carmen did not resemble her sister much. They had different coloring. Sofía had a light tan skin tone like their father, and Carmen was darker like their mother. They took her aside and drilled her with one more question:

"Where you going?"

"Guadalajara." They did not ask her anything else, but then two Retenes pulled Carmen over to the other side and asked her similar questions all the while trying to stump her.

"Where did you come from?"

"Puebla"

"Who are you with?"

"My sister."

"Where are you going?"

"Guadalajara."

Casually, they directed Carmen to get back on the bus and point out her seat. It was another trick to see if she was indeed Sofía's sister. If her story was truthful, sisters would naturally sit next to each other.

After what seemed like a really long time, the Retenes were able to piece together the two sister's responses and let them be. Sofía was quick to observe that not everyone was questioned at this stop—fortunately, only the ones who had been randomly selected. The bus was allowed to drive onward. That entire event lasted about an hour. To the girls, it seemed like an eternity.

Once everyone was settled back on the bus and it got on the road again, Sofía sat processing this latest event. *Another stop. Each one has its scary moments. How many more will there be?* At that moment, she overheard two of the passengers commenting about the ones who were questioned. She realized, to her surprise, an additional coyote was seated on that bus with them. *He's been pretending he was a passenger! He's been observing every aspect of the interrogation by the Retenes. Now I get it!*

She said to Carmen, "They keep their identity unknown unless something goes wrong, and that is why several travelers have called him by different names. It's true what Jessica said, in case they get stopped by border patrol, the coyotes will pretend to be migrants."

Carmen whispered, "Yeah, I noticed that too. Once we re-grouped, the guy with the blue shirt turned to the passengers with the same tone, emphasis and mannerisms as the other guides we've dealt with so far, and told them how pleased he was." He said, "You all did really well!"

Sofía sat back. *He was a coyote in-training who was taking the trip to learn the route and discover any obstacles for a future run. That is how they stay strong and the connections run so smoothly.* She was proud of her investigative work.

Chapter Eleven

Links in a Chain

Q. Is Guadalajara safe for migrants? How far is it from the US Border?

A. Guadalajara, the largest city in the Mexican State of Jalisco, is one of the most popular tourist destinations where territorial battles between criminal groups, kidnapping and violent gang activity are also common. The link between Guadalajara and the US is approximately 21 hr. 7 min or 1,288 miles.

It was now the fifth day since the girls had departed. The tour bus pulled over to add gasoline. They had arrived in Jalisco. Sofía had been comparing and analyzing each of the coyotes along the way.

Who are these guides? Why do they help migrants to cross the border? Sometimes, the person can be like a leader in charge of the travelers, like the drivers. Or he could be the guide who genuinely gets involved with explaining the details, like Michael. Or he could be the semi-hospitable rancher whose purpose is to let migrants stay the night to make some money. And sometimes, he can be like an important banker, just an anonymous person with a checklist of duties like the one who took mom's down payment. I wonder, do they get enjoyment or sense of purpose out of this? They all seem to be doing business together, like links in a chain of people who make up the entire plan. Each link in the chain is important in making the next step work. Like on a microscopic level looking down. She chuckled to herself. *They might look like tiny ants scurrying back and forth—each one with a job to do. I wonder which piece of the journey has the stronger links and which has the weaker links? And what happens if a link in the chain gets broken? It seems like everyone has a role, an agenda, and a desire to succeed—whatever that means to them. And within this intricately connected operation...all the links seem to be motivated by purpose, money, and time. Yes, the synchronization of time seems to be very important, like the scurrying of ants to get the job done.*

Breaking her thoughts, the bus driver interrupted, "You guys can shower and get food, but do it quickly! I don't see any Retenes around yet, so all is good. We only have maybe two hours to spare, and there are several of you, so don't linger. Be prepared to depart soon."

Sofía was relieved that everyone was allowed to get off the bus. That meant more safety and room to breathe, at least for a while. Before she got off the bus, the time had come to retrieve her hidden money. They were hungry. She went into the bathroom and delicately ripped the top lining of her underwear. They needed the Mexican money to eat and to use the shower facilities. She and Carmen noticed a small motel and diner very close by where travelers could buy Mexican food. She could tell this driver had been here before because she watched him make a beeline for the diner.

There were about ten shower stalls lined up near where the bus had parked, much like the ones she had seen at a beach resort. A lady about 45 years-old was standing ready. She said nothing, only watched each of the travelers as they got off the bus. She was waiting there to charge per person to use the showers. A sign made it clear to the travelers as they passed by, "If you want to use the toilet, you have to pay for that too." *Another person in the chain,* she deduced.

Anticipating arrivals, the lady had toiletries displayed and ready if anyone needed them: shampoo, soap, razors, wash-cloths, etc. Sofía inquired and learned that a quick, cold shower cost about twenty Mexican pesos, or five US dollars. Either currency was accepted, but Sofía thought, *It will be safer if I pay with the pesos as a 'Mexican' tourist.*

By now, it was routine between the girls to have one girl showering inside the stall while the others were outside guarding it. There was very little privacy and nothing but cold water. Since many people were in line, the lady spoke up and advised them not to take too long. After bathing, Carmelita was behaving almost like her old self again from the fresh shower. Carmen convinced Sofía to risk the walk and go into the diner next door to get her something nutritious to eat. Sofía agreed that they all could use something nutritious because she was getting tired of the crackers.

They bought two plates of Mexican food to share with the baby. There wasn't much to choose from, so they ordered Coca-Cola to drink along with a breakfast of chilaquiles. Sofía watched as the cook dished up the food. It was different than the Guatemalan chilaquiles their mom made. This Mexican breakfast dish had fresh tortilla chips simmered in salsa and topped with queso fresco, refried beans, and white rice. Their mom's was made from eggs, corn tortillas and queso fresco. But, for an extra 20 pesos, they asked to have it sprinkled with the Guatemalan herb, epazote. They really wanted it to taste like home. The only problem was neither anticipated how extremely hot and heavily spiced the food would be.

Carmen took a small bite. "What a mistake I've made again! I can't believe how much they used." She understood epazote to be poisonous if one consumed too much, so unfortunately felt the meal was not safe for Carmelita. She didn't dare let her eat it and was disappointed in herself. Both Sofía and Carmen declined to eat it, even though they were starving. All Sofía could think about was the money they had just wasted. They had spent nearly all of it. Soon they noticed one of the Ecuadorian girls, Sheila, heading toward them. Without hesitation, Sofía and Carmen walked over and gave her the plates of food as another 'thank you' for being able to use her cell phone.

Sofía whispered to Carmen, "It's OK. We'll survive. The sodas will have to suffice."

Three hours went by quickly. Like a cowboy directing a herd of cows, the driver whistled and made some noise for the travelers to return to the bus. They were getting closer to their destination. Anticipating it wouldn't be long now, they were instructed to leave behind any larger bags carrying their tell-tale migrant belongings; they were to lighten their load at each subsequent stop from now on, ditching any sweaty or wrinkly clothing for a fresh, clean appearance. It was imperative that they modeled tourist behavior.

After just half an hour into their ride, Sofía heard a loud exploding sound and felt the bus rocking. Carmen looked out the window. The bus was crooked, leaning over to one side. Some of the passengers shouted, "Flat tire!"

The wheel did indeed come off the bus. The passengers were frustrated. The obstacles seemed to increase the closer they got to their journey's end. Sofía thought, *Now what?*

Luckily, they were near a gas station. The driver ordered everyone to "*Stay* on the bus!" and he got off to investigate.

Through the tipped window, Carmen and Sofía watched with surprise as the people, probably the true tourists, descended the bus. Sofía said "Many of the passengers aren't paying any mind to what we were told. They're getting off to inspect for themselves. This is risky...it's going to draw attention to us."

They observed. One by one, the tourists entered the gas station and bought snacks, drinks, and candy. The scene of scurrying ants on a mission came to Sofía's mind again. Still hungry and unable to follow the rules, Carmen decided she would sneak off the bus. She convinced Sofía that in a fast-five minutes, she could get something for the baby—anything that was not spicy hot and not smothered in epazote.

Carmen flew down the aisle and was off the bus in seconds. She rushed directly into the store and stood patiently in line with the others. The hot dogs caught her attention, so she bought two with the remaining coins she had left from Sofía's money. As promised, Carmen was back on the bus in less than five minutes. There was no way she wanted to run after another bus like she had done the night before.

Meanwhile, the driver had stowed on board the exact tools he needed to fix the flat. He knew exactly what to do and went to work right away, swiftly and efficiently. He was able to repair the tire himself in less than 30 minutes. Like clockwork, nobody broke a link in the chain.

With everyone safely back on the bus, they drove for the rest of the day. Sofía was not comfortable at all. She was restless, hungry, and tired from sitting all day. Hour after hour, they were squeezed together in the seat with no room to move or stretch or walk around. They extended their arms every now and then, as best they could. Everyone spoke very softly. Time was going by so slowly now. She napped for about two hours, but then, it was pure boredom. They were all antsy. Sofía guarded the tiny purse-like bag on her lap which had the last of their personal items. Carmen held her napping baby.

Now that she had time to ruminate about the the whole situation, almost from a birds-eye view looking down at the ants that scurried to form the links in the journey from beginning to end, Sofía's emotions were gearing up again. She had nothing to distract her thoughts. She questioned what she was doing in this place at this moment. She asked herself thousands of questions: *If I were home, what would I be doing now, in my own country? What is going to happen to me? What if we get sent back? What if something terrible happens to us? What will happen tomorrow? What will my life be like when I get there? Will I be able to go to school? Get a job? When will I ever see my country again? What will my aunt be like when I get there? Will she be like my mother? When will I see my mom or my family?*

Her thoughts always came back to the fear of the unknown. Sofía liked to play it safe. She preferred to stay quiet, listening and observing others—never revealing. Many feelings of sadness, nervousness, regret, and uneasiness ran through her. She considered the events of these last few days and nights, with thoughts of the unfamiliar, far from her family, and the comforts she missed from home. She missed her mom. She missed the food, and it had only been a few days. She did not want to share her thoughts and feelings for fear of spoiling the plan everyone had so carefully put in motion, even though she truly wanted to support her sister. Her thoughts became more depressing as the journey became her reality.

She thought, *At least Carmen could be distracted and focus on her baby.* The uncertainty of it all made her brain work on overtime as she sat there very still, looking straight ahead, alone in her thoughts.

Chapter Twelve

A Stop at Destiny

Q. Can one moment in time change the trajectory of your

future?

A. Absolutely, it only takes one.

At about 10:00 that night, they drove by another Reten station where all passing cars, buses, and freight trucks were mandated to stop. The coyote had explained earlier that depending on where in the country they were located and how many officers were employed at any particular station, each one seemed to have their own routine and style of conducting the inspection. It had been droned into their heads from the start: Retenes work for the Mexican Immigration Office and therefore have the power to send a traveler packing instantly if they think a person is a foreigner.

Sofía repeated to herself, *Follow the rules, obey their commands, and keep silent...but when you must, speak like a Mexican*.

This time, a Mexican policeman boarded their bus and pointed to several people. "You, you and you, *get off*!!" Scouting intently at the people, he calmly and very slowly made his way down the aisle of the bus. Of course, he pointed to Sofía to get off too. With sweaty palms and nerves about to explode, she hoped her pounding heart would not beat so loud to attract his attention.

As he approached her seat, he repeated his command. "*You!*" He lit up her face with a flashlight.

Sofía kept thinking, *Please not me...Maybe point at someone else...Please don't pick me!*

But he pointed the flashlight right in her face as he repeated his order for her to get off the bus.

Nooooo not again! Why?! Why am I singled out? I have done everything right. Why me? Is it because we're sitting in the last seat of the bus?

Sofía's eyes met Carmen's with a quick glance, and even in the dark, her sister could read the emotions on her face. Carmen motioned with her hand to 'calm down' as she mouthed the words to her, "Cálmate." "Calm down."

The angels must have heard them because, by the grace of God this time, little Carmelita remained sleeping throughout the inspection and did not call attention to the officer. As Sofía stood up to exit the bus, she thought, *More than likely Carmen was not singled out because she always had the baby in her arms.* Nevertheless, she stood tall, took a deep breath through her nose, and inched her way down the aisle and off the bus. *I must remain silent. My name is Isabela. Remember your dialect. Keep silent. Will they search me, believe me, send me home without my sister? Here we go again...*

Standing still, Sofía looked around nervously. She had a habit now of counting the surrounding people at all times. She counted ten passengers chosen to step off the bus. Each one had an officer assigned who would interrogate their intentions for travel. She felt the wet sweat coming from her armpits and remembered what the first coyote told them about sweating and knew—this was not good.

Once again, the officer was quick to ask her name and the usual questions—

"Where are you going?"

She answered, "Guadalajara." She picked her nails from the nervousness.

The Reten noticed her behavior and asked her why she was fidgeting with her fingers. Confused, not realizing that she had indeed been fidgeting with her nails, she answered, "Because you asked me to get off!" She didn't know what else to say.

He retorted with a smile, "You know I can send you back to your country?"

By his tone, Sofía was convinced. No doubt *he knew* she was not from Mexico. She responded with a softer nervousness, almost flirt-like smile back at him. She didn't know what else to say. He wrote her name down in a booklet.

She smiled again and gently asked, "Can I use the bathroom?" From the corner of her eye, she could see they were standing near the outdoor port-a-potties, lined up in a row for use by the travelers.

He smiled back, "Go", and accompanied her to one. As he walked by her side, Sofía looked up enough to notice just how many more people had been stopped from other buses traveling past this station. As they made their way, eyes still focused downward, and the Reten close by her side, she sensed all the chaos and movement. There were at least two other buses full of people and many cars with dozens of policemen scattered around. Sniffing dogs were doing their job. She surmised, *This has to be the last stop before the border.*

Taking a deep, profound breath, she entered the bathroom and began to pray. *Please God, I need to calm down and think—How can I get out of this?* Her eyes closed, she inhaled deeply again, then exhaled a long, relaxing breath. All of a sudden, a calmness came over her. She waited a few short minutes, straightened her clothes, held her head up, and walked out.

The officer was still there waiting. He kept staring at her. He was not an older Reten; he was a young man of about 29 years old. Finally, he asked, "Are you done? Are you ready?"

She responded, "Yeah," like it was an everyday occurrence. He motioned to her with his eyes letting her know, he realized she was indeed, not Mexican. He gestured to her with a nod and a quick touch on her shoulder, indicating to get back on the bus.

Sofía's eyes met his for just a split second but they quickly looked away, walking as fast as she could toward the bus. She did not want to waste any time. *Is he letting me go? Why? Don't ask! Keep Silent. Don't look back. For now, he's a link that is imperative to making the next step viable for us. He's a compassionate human who perhaps pities me, feels empathy, or maybe just feels our struggle—at this moment in time. That's all I need to believe.* She would analyze this moment later and accept that one moment would have changed the trajectory of her future.

Once she boarded the bus, she looked around and counted how many seats were empty. *How many people were retained?* She had been studying everyone's faces and remembered them. She had seen who got off and realized there were three of them who didn't get back on. Three out of the ten travelers had been retained.

An enormous sense of victory filled her senses as she sat down in her seat. A flood of relief came over her. She grabbed her sister's hand and thought, *It was a miracle I didn't get sent back.* She closed her eyes for a moment and began to pray. She put her hand on her chest and thought, *Well, the three of us are still together. We are still on our way.* She looked up at the clock sitting on the dashboard of the bus. Their red numerals shone in the darkness. All of this happened in twenty-nine minutes.

Retenes closed the compartment doors under the bottom part of the bus. The final few outside noises from the dogs that had sniffed the stored suitcases for drugs dissipated. Seconds later, they felt the bus gearing up to go. The whispering amongst the remaining migrant passengers broke loose:

"There were fifteen who started with us on this bus."

"Which ones got retained?"

"Who is still with us?"

"How many mandatory stops do you think we have left?"

There was something favorable about the people who were 'the real' Mexican tourists sitting on the bus with them. They sat quietly and listened to the chatter. Even though they were keen on what was going on with the migrants who were trying to flee through their country—and had several opportunities by now to speak up and turn them in—they never did. They, too, were an empathetic and an important link in the chain.

The bus drove until the morning dawn. Sofía estimated they were on the bus about 30 hours. Carmelita slept while Carmen and Sofía chatted endlessly about their discoveries and observations up till this point. As they quietly scrolled through the events from the last few days, they were able to muster a few laughs at Carmelita's way of inciting the others with her cough, the cell phone they left behind, when the scary Retenes asked Sofía to get off the bus, and the dreadful food. They also began to express out loud to each other their future predictions about the new life that awaited them across the border.

Carmen asked, "Do you think Aunt Martina will look much like mom?"

Without hesitation, Sofía replied, "As long as she can cook like mom, I think it's going to be great."

"Do you think her house will be anything like ours from back home?"

Sofía shook her head, "I doubt it. I think she'll have lots of Guatemalan pictures and knick-knacks around to remember her roots. Somehow I think it will be a huge house—really big with lots of rooms and fun things to do...I wonder if her children can speak Spanish? I'm excited…They can help us learn English, for sure!"

Carmen looked down at Carmelita and nodded her head, "Yeah, English is so important. We need to learn English to be able to do anything going forward. I think we'll learn it real fast. Thank God Carmelita will grow up knowing both languages. Thank God they are willing to sponsor us, because we would never have this opportunity otherwise without their support."

Sofía agreed, "Family is everything."

Remarkably every day, in every event, they had experienced luck. They chatted in disbelief about how they came through everything with blessings. Whether it was Karma, a fluke, serendipity, or destiny…whatever one chose to call it, they felt grateful as everything fell into place. Sofía looked out the window into the darkness. *No, nothing bad so far. I wonder why some people have not been so fortunate. I hope our luck doesn't end any time soon. I don't understand why some are successful and others have to suffer. I wish I knew all the rules.* As she drifted into a light sleep, she smiled. *I hope our future continues to show us lucky breaks and triumphant, happy endings.* It was clear, they had to acknowledge just how blessed they had been.

The Yellow Taxi

Q. What do you get when a white house on the left is across from a pink and white taxi on the right?

A. You get a lot of confusion and an awaiting yellow taxi.

By now, it was almost 5:00 AM, still dark and very quiet outside as the sun rose. The bustle of the day was still a few hours away. Their tourist bus approached the last Reten station before the border. It came to a slow stop. This time, two Mexican police came aboard with flashlights and casually checked over the passengers, one by one. But this time, nobody was told to get off. They asked only a few for identification as they wandered down the aisle.

Sofía faked like she was sleeping, tilting her head on to her shoulder, hoping they would not pick her out. Carmen breastfed the baby, hoping to remain insignificant. With her eyes shut tight, Carmen hoped and prayed that Carmelita would remain still and not call their attention. She put a cloth diaper over her shoulder, covering Carmelita's face, and she, too, faked like she was sleeping.

The policemen stopped when they got to Carmen's seat. Two tall men in uniforms stood there looking down at her. Silence filled the bus. Nobody stirred. Sofía peered out of the corner of her eye as discreetly as she could. She noticed that one of the policemen had focused on Carmen. Sofía moved ever so slightly to get out of the way. She did *not* want to give them a reason to question her, nor did she want a repeat from the last stop. She prayed, *Please don't let Carmen be next.*

He saw Sofía shift and within a nano-second, shined the flashlight on her face. Sofía feared it was coming. She held on tight, reeling in her thoughts that wanted to race ahead of her. She continued to assume the phony sleeping position. She dared not open her eyes and wondered, *How do actors do it?* As destiny would have it, the two men turned around and sauntered back to the bus door. They did not say a thing. To everyone's surprise, not one traveler was removed.

Keeping score, Sofía noted this inspection lasted under ten minutes. She swore she heard exhales from every passenger on board. She felt the tension release and heard the many sighs of relief as the two Retenes descended the steps down off the bus.

Back on the road again, they drove on for about one hour leaving Santa Ana in the rear-view mirror. They were certainly closer to the border after driving all night. Sofía was more than hungry. After experiencing three Reten stops, by now she and Carmelita were starving. Carmen never ate much. There were no gas station stops, no cold showers, no food, and Carmelita was fed up with being on the bus. That pitiful hot dog only lasted them so long. Carmelita began to cry, calling attention to herself once again.

Still kind of dark outside, the bus came to a sudden jerky stop. Sofía counted. Six travelers disembarked. Carmen whispered, "Are these the ones who are going to cut through the desert to cross the border?"

"Yeah."

Sofía remembered they would be going that way because she recalled Miguel telling them that at a certain point, 'six' would leave them for the more risky trek on foot from there on out. She didn't know which ones specifically until she saw them get off. She thought of her uncle and all the stories about going through the desert. *With God's blessing and perhaps Saint Jame's too, they will be successful. Now I understand why they opted to cut through the desert. Even though it's more dangerous, if they make it through, they will avoid having the unnerving experience of being stopped by the Retenes!*

Sofía revisited the numbers again. It was a way to keep her mind occupied. She kept track of each of the passenger's faces, their belongings, their agendas, and their whereabouts. *There were 15 migrants on this bus: three were retained at one of the stops, then six—three women and three men—were let out to cross the desert, and now there are six.*

She remembered overhearing one of the pretend-tourists say, "All the ones who were with Miguel are going to the desert." It made sense to her now. *Another link. For sure he was another coyote because how else would he have known Miguel so well?* Still bothered though, she thought, *Why would any woman want to take a chance in the desert? This is scary enough!*

Ten or fifteen minutes later, they arrived at their last stop. The remaining migrants were told to disembark the tourist bus. The driver confirmed that Sofía, Carmen, Carmelita, a young twelve-year-old boy named Santiago, the El Salvadoran woman Jessica and her baby would be next to leave.

He gave them explicit instructions, "Listen very carefully. When you get off, you will see a white house on the left side of the street. Directly in front of that there will be a *yellow* taxi. There will be a new coyote driving the taxi. Get into the taxi and follow his directions. Do not get confused or swayed. There will be other pink and yellow taxis around clamoring for your attention. Do not speak to anyone! Do *not* get into any other vehicle."

It all happened so fast. Sofía panicked. *Oh boy… Which color was which? What did he say again? He spoke too fast! What if we get the colors mixed up?* Under her breath, she repeated, *Yellow, on the left, yellow, yellow on the left.*

The tourist bus stopped, and six got off. There was a white taxi with a pink-colored roof across the street. The driver waved to them. To the right were three yellow taxis parked in a row, next to a brown car. One of the drivers motioned to them. But when she looked to the left, exactly as they were told, Sofía spotted the white bus with a yellow taxi in front of it. Hopefully, waiting for them. That driver made no movement, only a slight nod. All six marched in line toward the yellow taxi on the left. None veered off into a different direction. With a slight sense of relief, Sofía knew it had to be correct. All six got into the yellow taxi on the left.

The driver identified himself as Edwin. He was around forty-seven years old, fat, and ugly. He had pock marks all over his face, a black mustache, and smelled of sweat. He told them they were going to a small hotel about five minutes away. Edwin walked them straight into the hotel, right past the check-in desk. Close together, they went directly into their hotel room.

Sofía linked more pieces of the chain together. Because this was now obviously all prearranged, they did not have to pay or officially check-in. Their room was kitty-corner to the main office of the hotel. *How convenient,* she speculated, *The boss of all the links in the chain probably owned this hotel and the vehicles we traveled in, too. I bet he bribes some of the Retenes along the way as well!*

It had one small bed, a bathroom with no door, and one small window with the shade pulled down to block anyone from looking in. It had a stove with a ceramic can of beans on it, a fridge with no shelves but was packed with cans of soda and corn tortillas. There were garbage bags of old, dirty clothes stuffed in it. The sun was coming up and the neighboring roosters were crowing loudly as if to announce their arrival.

Edwin disclosed the next part of the plan. "In a little while, I'm going to call my connections to alert them that you are all here. In turn, they will contact each of your families to let them know you have arrived this far. Your family will then pay the rest of the money owed. When I hear back that your part has been paid, then I will take you to the border when there is an opportune time to cross. From there, you are on your own to cross over."

Sofía thought about how complicated and how complex this entire trip must have been to organize, yet it was running like clock-work. She thought about how many others had done this before her. If there were hiccups along the way, such as the flat tire, there was always a "plan B" in place, ready to be executed. She was amazed at the thought of just how many people were involved right from the beginning, so many links to the chain.

She was not sure why, but Edwin lined them up and sat them down on the bed. He made sure the young boy Santiago sat the furthest away from himself and proceeded to sit down next to Jessica, who was trying to accommodate her baby. Straight away, he touched the girl on her breast and began rubbing her leg. Then, he ordered Santiago to move even further away from everyone, so he could not see what Edwin was planning to do.

Alarmed, Sofía looked at her sister with fear. As he continued to caress Jessica's leg, Edwin spoke to them in a degrading way. As if to have a double meaning, he muttered, "You girls are disgusting and need clean clothes and a shower because you're *dirty*!" Jessica repeatedly pushed his hands away as he spoke. He continued in a tone that insinuated authority, "I'll give you clothes and you'll give me sex in return."

Sofía shook her head in disbelief and looked down. *Miguel had warned us that something like this might happen.* She thought about how obnoxious and disrespectful he was—quite different from the others so far. Jessica did not say a word to him but continued to put her baby on her lap to push off his hand. Sofía could see that her fellow traveler was otherwise frozen stiff in shock, while she and Carmen were speechless too.

The boy Santiago refused to look away as ordered. Santiago was young but fearless to this man. His intention was to not let the women alone with a perverted man. Watching Santiago stand up to him assured the girls that when you have someone traveling with you who is on your team, it bridges the gaps and creates tighter bonds and connections. She remembered the old man who offered Carmelita candy. *These group-loyalties are created by small, accidental events that bind us together. They are good links.*

Not having much luck with his advancements toward Jessica, Edwin motioned to Carmen. He insisted then that she would have to go with him into town and get fresh clothes. He gave strict instructions that only one person could leave the hotel room at a time.

All the while the taxi driver spoke, he tried hard to intimidate the young migrants. With stolen confidence, Edwin assured them, "Do you even know how *easily* I can get you sent back?" His words played mind-games, as he did his best to take advantage of the moment. Reminding them of their captive situation, he arrogantly let them know he held the upper hand. "Look how *far* from your homes you are, and *how long* you've traveled to get here! Do you realize how much money was spent on *you*, and the *debt* your family has acquired just so that you could be here? Do you know just how close to the border you are now? You *need* me. Are you willing to throw it all away by disobeying me?" He cautioned them with his sinister laugh, "Don't let this all be for nothing," and reiterated, "Shortly, your families will be paying the rest of the money, so you better act grateful."

Sofía never took her eyes off Carmen and Carmelita as she silently prayed away. *I can't believe that of all the people in the chain who had helped us, this taxi guy Edwin would be so unscrupulous. How dare he try to scare us into doing what he wants in the form of sexual assaults. He is disgusting!*

With the stores opening shortly, Carmen agreed to go into town with him to buy them all clean clothes. Now that they were so close, fresh clothes were necessary to avoid calling attention to themselves as traveling migrants. Carmen got up and went into the bathroom. Santiago and then Sofía stood in front of the doorway as she ripped open the seam of her underwear and took out the 600 pesos, about 33 US dollars, sewn in there. It was the absolute last of their emergency money.

Petrified, Sofía whispered to Carmen, "Promise me, you will shout and scream as loud as you can if Edwin tries to do something to you while you're out. *Please* be careful! Be willing to call for the police even if it means we must go back to Guatemala! I am OK with that. I'd rather go back before giving in to Edwin's advances."

Armed with Sofía's words, Carmen left the baby with her sister while she and Edwin went to get the fresh, clean clothes they needed.

Sure enough, Edwin tried to touch Carmen in the car ride to the store.

He told her, "Once we enter the store, you're going to pretend you are my woman." He demanded in his sleazy way, "You'll kiss me and hold my hand like you are my girlfriend. You must do this or they will suspect you are a migrant."

Carmen knew immediately it was a trick. She responded firmly with furrowed eyebrows, "If you *try* to do anything, I will *scream* and call out for the police." She made it clear to him and stated in no uncertain terms, "I don't care if I make it to the border or not. I will *not* put up with your dirty actions."

Now that his attempts had failed, he then offered to pay Carmen some pesos for sex. He tried to convince her, "You need the money. This is the *only* way you are going to make it. Trust me."

Remaining silent, tiny Carmen refused to dignify his offer with a response.

They parked his taxi next to the store. She had enough money to buy clothes for herself, Carmelita, and Sofía. There should be just enough money left to buy some food. Right next to the clothing store was the usual street vendor, a make-shift diner. She brought back enough chicken and rice for everyone, anticipating they would all be starving.

Once back at the hotel, Edwin wasted no time to warn the group with a threatening voice, "Don't you *dare* ever tell *anyone* what happened in the car ride or in this hotel room. *If* you do, I will come after you and make sure you get sent back—or I will *kill* you! I will make your family back home *pay the price.*"

It was obvious he was coercing them into believing that no one, including those in the United States, should be aware of his existence or his role in 'helping' migrants cross the border. But they all realized the reason for Edwin's threats: if they *did* tell anyone how he treated them, *he* would lose his job...or one of the links would kill *him*.

After his bully-speech and refusing to give up, Edwin ordered Santiago to go into the hotel room next door. It was evident he believed his threats were scaring them. He attempted once again to get sexual favors from the girls. But the boy shook his head and stood his ground. He refused to go. Santiago had suspected the dirty old man wanted to be alone with the girls. He instinctively knew Edwin would take advantage of their vulnerability. Even though he was only twelve, Santiago would not leave the girls alone. They remained huddled together on the bed and ate the chicken. The six travelers stuck together and ignored the coyote.

Sofía whispered to the others, "How ironic is it for him to say the danger is 'out there,' when the real danger is inside this hotel room with *him*."

Carmen replied, "I called him a nasty, dirty old man! Thank goodness the store was close to the hotel and the ride with him went quickly. At least the food was cheap and we all get to eat before we cross today." The others agreed.

After eating, they needed to shower, change into their new clothes, and get ready for the final border crossing. The problem: there was no bathroom door to close. This was strategic on Edwin's part—ensuring the see-through plastic shower curtain was visible to him from the rest of the room. If the girls went into the bathroom, he could peek at them.

"Hey dumb kid, leave them alone! They need to take a shower! Get out of the way!" Edwin watched as the girls went into the bathroom.

"No! I'm not leaving them." Santiago stuck to his guns and flatly, but politely, refused to leave the room with the girls. Instead, he devised an idea to take the bedspread off the bed and use it to cover the transparent shower curtain. Santiago said astutely, "I respect women and their privacy, and I'm *not* leaving." He stood tall before the bathroom door, protecting them from the taxi driver's dirty, piercing eyes. And with that pronouncement, the old, fat, ugly coyote finally left the hotel room to call his connection and officially report the arrival of the six near the border. The girls cleaned up the food plates, and bathed in peace, thanks to Santiago.

As they got ready, Jessica recounted the story about the last time she made it this close to the border. "I had made friends with another girl named Emily. She was about twenty years old from Guatemala. We traveled almost the entire way together with a small group of people. But when we got near the border, we don't know why, a man approached her and she walked away with him. She never came back. About two hours later, they found her dead. Her hands and feet were tied. It was awful. I had her ID in my things, so I had to call her mother and tell her the horrific news."

There was a long silence. "But" Jessica said, with mustered enthusiasm, "This time we're all going to make it. I just know it."

Edwin returned close to noon to say that Sofía's family was the first to pay up. Betina had deposited the money. Carmen and Sofía would be the first to leave the hotel. Santiago and Jessica's payment had not successfully gone through yet, so they were going to have to wait a few more hours. Edwin was ready to escort Sofía, Carmen, and the baby to the border and would return to get the others once their families had paid up.

Edwin scoffed as if he were indifferent to the situation. He explained the plan for the border: "I'm going to drive you in my taxi and drop you off in front of the wall—your final destination. This is a cash on delivery operation. We are only paid when there is a successful border crossing. There is going to be a big, round, broken hole in the wall where you climb through to get to the other side. US Immigration Officers will be waiting on the other side. They will probably notice you immediately and come and get you as soon as you cross over. Not far from there is the US Immigration Building. That is where they'll take you to process you into the United States."

With that, he told the others to "*Stay put*" and he would be back shortly.

Chapter Fourteen

The Border

Q. How effective is the wall at the US Southern Border?

A. In 2017, construction was ordered for replacement and repair of fences. New barriers, some of which were 30 ft. high, were built in places where previously there were none. Effectiveness is inconclusive.

A creepy feeling came over Sofía. *How will we know if he's telling the truth? How will we know if it's true that our mother has successfully paid the money? Is this another sly attempt on Edwin's part to sexually assault one of us—or both of us? Would he really physically harm us? Will we end up dead too?*

She and Carmen looked at each other and wondered if they could trust him. Sofía said, "I believe this might be a ploy to separate us from the others. If you feel safe enough, then I'll trust your intuition."

"Don't worry, I know what to do if that is the case," Carmen replied under her breath. So with a quick glance to the others and shout out to the Man Upstairs, they agreed to leave with the disgusting taxi driver.

Sofía whispered back to Carmen, "I'm sure we are about five-ten minutes away from the wall. Let's see how long it takes him to drive us there. If we drive any longer than that, then—Plan B—just in case, we'll both scream because we know he's not taking us to the border."

Meanwhile, as they said their quick farewells, Jessica and Santiago assured them they also had a plan. "We made a pact to stay together, and when it is our turn to leave for the border, we will leave together. That way, no one will ever be alone with Edwin. We, too, are willing to scream for the police before we would give in to sexual assaults and secrecy to protect *him*." Sofía smiled with a sigh of relief.

Moments later and sweating profusely, Sofía and Carmen, with Carmelita on her hip, walked out of the hotel into the hot late afternoon sun. They leaped into his taxi, nervous and emotional, yet full of wonder at what would happen next. Edwin directed them again, "Do not forget, when I drop you off, look for the open hole in the wall. That is where you are going to cross over to the US."

Sofía kept an eye on the time. He drove exactly thirteen minutes and said, "I'm slowing down now because we're here."

He slowed the car to a crawl as he approached the usual drop off spot. The car stopped within feet from where they were supposed to get out. Glancing out the taxi window, they witnessed, to their complete surprise, that the hole had been fully covered up with fairly fresh cement. There was no longer a hole! It had been repaired. Surrounding it was a new and solid wall made of tall steel slats that were reinforced with concrete and re-bar. It had newly placed barbed wire enveloping the top of the beams. You couldn't see through it or over to the other side.

Edwin panicked. He did not know it had been closed since his last drop off. Inching his way further down the road, he drove at a snail's pace. Cautiously, he was looking and wishing for another opening. As he did so, he noticed in his rear-view mirror the Mexican Border Police following closely behind his taxi. All at once, the lights flashed, the police sounded the sirens, and with a megaphone, they ordered him to pull over.

An additional police car blockade formed just up ahead of them. His car would soon need to come to a full stop. Edwin noticed two big pieces of slightly stacked cement near the newly repaired wall. He urged the girls to take off, shouting, "Now! Beat it! Get out! Get out *now* and *jump* the wall yourselves! Go!" He paused to reassess the situation, then continued to holler, "Go girls, Go! You can jump up on that block of cement, then jump over the wall yourselves. And hurry because here come the police!"

Past stories of border crossings flashed through Sofía's head. She remembered how others described where they had crossed, the way they had crossed over, and what she would encounter: *You just walk! You'll be able to cross easily. Someone opens a gate and you can go through...Hah! What a joke!* she thought. She scolded herself for believing those people. All this time she had imagined some kind of gate with people entering the US by walking through it. *A Gate!*

She refocused. *This is no time for jokes. I never imagined we would make it to the end, only to find a solid six-foot wall we need to jump over! Lies! Nobody ever mentioned I'd have to scale a wall that's topped with barbed wire. That's not how it's supposed to be...This was not part of the plan!*

She had anticipated there might be something to it besides a gate. Still, she learned for the first time from Miguel that life would be hard once they got to the US. That was a complete shock. *Nobody ever discussed the possibility that the border would be a tall wall that would be difficult, if not impossible, to get over. What else don't I know about?*

But there was no time to think anymore. She glanced at the tall wall and the words burst out, *Oh my God, how can we do this?* She wondered, *What was Edwin thinking?* Looking around, she knew there was no way she, nor her tiny sister Carmen, were tall enough. *Even if we could, how would we get the baby over?*

Edwin hollered back one last time as they sat frozen in the back seat, "*Go*! If they catch you now, they will send you back. Go jump where that block of cement is raised up, or the police will get you here!"

They carried only a small sack with the baby bottle, a few pampers, and a tiny blanket. There was nothing else to carry or worry about. The police sirens were getting louder. Edwin drove so slowly until, without any further hesitation, they jumped out of his taxi. In seconds, he maneuvered around the barricade and was gone.

They stared at the wall for a split-second and realized the police were right behind them with flashing lights. Sofía still wondered, *How?*

There was a plank of cement in front of them, leaning up against the wall. Without wasting another second, Carmen sprang into action. She set the baby down and ran over to make a bridge with her hands. She called out to her sister, "You first!" She motioned to hoist Sofía up the solid mural wall with its dangerous barbed wires wrapping around to greet them.

Sofía jumped on top of the plank and grabbed a hold of one of the strong re-bars that stuck out. She put her foot in Carmen's hand and when Carmen gave a big heave, up she went. Her pants and foot got caught. She heard the sound of ripping pants, but over she went. Her hands were covered with blood from vaulting over the top and one shoe landed on the ground. It didn't matter. She made it.

This isn't a dress rehearsal. It's finally happening," she thought as she shook her head in disbelief. Safely on the other side now, she had landed on her back when she made sense of their words. She felt a little dizzy but screamed out to Carmen, "The bag with pampers and the blanket broke my fall!"

The flashing lights and sirens were still going louder and stronger. The border police had gotten out of their vehicle and swiftly approached Carmen. With their white megaphones, they repeated the warnings "Get down. Get down from there *now*! You know this is illegal. We are the police!"

Carmen replied, "Get up! Grab the baby!" Carmen's words woke Sofía from the dizziness, and she stood up. Carmen said again, "*Grab her, grab her!*"

Sofía looked up and responded, "There is a massive wall between us." Sofía could not see Carmen, and Carmen could not see Sofía.

"How can I see her? I can't see! Where are you? How do I know where to catch her? If I miss, she will fall to her death!" There was no time to think. They had come so far. Sofía screamed back to her sister again, "Where are you?"

Carmen did not wait for her to answer. Estimating where Sofía had to be standing on the other side, she threw the baby up and over and said, "Here she comes! Catch her!"

There was no time to think. Sofía looked up as Carmelita was falling into her arms. She yelled out a profound cry and informed her sister, "I caught the baby! I caught the baby!" She set baby Carmelita down for a second and looked up.

Tiny Carmen, a bit taller and weighing a lot less than Sofía, had somehow hoisted herself up and came flying over the top. Sofía reached over and caught Carmen's foot just as she landed, just in time, to avoid falling on the baby. It was a miracle.

In just a few short minutes, the three of them were now on the other side. The police sirens and megaphone warnings began fading away. Gradually it became quiet. The sisters looked at each other and hugged tightly. Traumatized, Sofía repeated the words, "I caught the baby! I caught the baby!" She could not hold back the tears any longer, and fell to her knees crying. She looked up and gave thanks to God's mercy.

It was Sunday, February 12th, 2017. They picked up the baby, and the three of them, filled with emotions, sobbed away.

Minus the torn clothes and bloody cuts, they were thankful they made it safely to the other side. The three got up, still weeping, and walked arm in arm. Within two minutes, the United States Office of Immigration approached them. They wiped their tears, shook off the dirt, and took deep breaths, as they looked at each other wondering, "Now what?"

Chapter Fifteen

Waiting to be Released

Q. Why do people intimidate others?

A. Due to low self-esteem or insecurities, some people intentionally intimidate others in order to bully and manipulate, which then gives them a sense of confidence and assertiveness. It is important to remember that you're not always responsible for the feelings you inspire in others.

Minutes after Sofía, Carmen, and Carmelita had crossed the border into the United States, with barely enough time to stand up and brush themselves off, the US Border Patrol approached them. A barrage of questions came firing,

"What is your name? How old are you?"

Carmen replied, "Mi nombre es Carmen. Tengo dieciocho años." Sofía remained frozen.

"Where are you coming from?"

Carmen said, "Guatemala."

"Do you have any telephone numbers? Who knows you are here?"

They both remained silent. Sofía was overwhelmed. Neither she nor Carmen knew how to speak English well. They understood some words and guessed the rest. Responding as best they could, they pointed with their fingers, made gestures, and were very happy to answer all they could—honestly this time. No need to lie or hide anything, anymore.

On a tiny pad of paper, the men quickly wrote down what they heard and escorted them toward the border patrol office building. It was only a five-minute walk from where they landed. The girls glanced at each other and whispered unassumingly in Spanish, "They're probably immigration officials because they have *green* uniforms."

When they entered the building, Sofía's eyes wandered all around, up and down, here and there. She was mesmerized by such a large room. It was shaped like a huge rectangle, surrounded by many rooms on all sides. She was used to places with just one or two small, modest rooms. There were so many doors. *Uno, dos, tres, cuatro, cinco...ocho...doce...Díos mío! Tantas puertas!* She tried to count them all. Nothing of this gigantic space she encountered gave her clues to where they were or what was going on. They could not read any of the signs on the walls. They were told to sit on metal benches.

Before long, about five more border patrol officers in green uniforms encircled them. No other non-uniformed people around, which made Sofía nervous. She wondered, *Where were all the American people?*

Carmen and Sofía remained very quiet. One of the patrolmen went over to the water dispenser fountain and filled a cup with hot water. Neither of the girls had ever had soup from a cup like that before, but they were most grateful. They were starving, so it tasted good. Another man gave them a tiny box of fruit drink. Carmelita drank it down in a flash and coughed every now and then. She was still recovering from the virus symptoms she experienced on the trip.

Little by little, the officers went away, but two men remained with them asking questions. There were no women officers in sight. They asked the girls to remove all their outer clothing, including their shoes. They searched through the jackets, scrutinizing the blanket, and the small bag. Sofía watched curiously as they looked meticulously inside and out of each of the shoes.

Repeatedly they asked, "Is there anything else you have to show us?"

They had so little left with them by now. Sofía figured they were looking for contraband and continued to gesture with her shoulders, *I don't understand.*

Twenty minutes later, someone new entered the room. Instantly, the atmosphere changed. This man mainly spoke English but threw in some Spanish with a hard-to-understand accent. With his furrowed eyebrows, squinting eyes, and a deep, negative tone, he demanded to know, "Why are you guys here?" He repeated his question, only this time he said it much louder. "WHY ARE YOU HERE?"

Carmen spoke up. She tried her best to express the sentiment that she and her sister wanted a better life because of a lot of delinquency in her country. She went on hopelessly trying to explain in broken English, lots of hand gestures, and a heavy Guatemalan accent. "Mi novio hit me lot. Every day. He scream lot. He mother no me like. I no money. He kill me. He take baby. He hurt me. He drink. He make me work hard. I cry. Mi mama cry. I scare. Mi baby scare. No help...police no help. No care." She shook her head and looked down, "I no more..."

She knew it would be difficult for them to understand and more difficult for her to muster the correct way to express the abuse she suffered from the father of her child. She struggled to find the words but knew she had to keep going.

This man in the green uniform had zero patience to let her finish them. With an air of righteous confidence, the questions kept coming. Each question got louder and louder, "*DO YOU KNOW WHO DONALD J. TRUMP IS? DO YOU KNOW HE IS THE PRESIDENT OF THE UNITED STATES?*"

Carmen and Sofía were two young girls in a foreign country, but they immediately knew what discrimination felt like. His attitude was apparent with the increased volume.

Sofía's eyes fixated on the officer's hands. He had a way of putting them on his hips and sticking his fingers below the belt as he rocked forward and back. She looked up. He squeezed his lips together as he spoke. This increased her fear and she began to tremble. She didn't know if it was the cold air-conditioning blowing all over her body or if it was this man. She felt more panic at that moment than at any other time during the entire trip, including with Edwin the taxi driver.

The lecture droned on, citing why his president "didn't want *aliens* here." As if to brag of his country's virtues, he questioned and scolded them at the same time. "*You people* bring violence, drugs, and bad things to the Americans." He repeatedly told them they were "Bad people" and "They had *NO* right to be here." He called them aliens over and over. "Do you know it is *ILLEGAL* for aliens to cross the border? And do you know *I* can send you right back? I can send you right back to wherever you came from."

He is trying his hardest to scare us, Sofía thought, a*nd it's working because I'm really frightened*. She looked over to her sister the moment he paused. When her eyes met Carmen's, they confirmed to each other just how frightened they were. Tears began to stream down Carmen's face. Tired and defeated, Sofía thought, *Maybe she hadn't explained well. Maybe they don't care?*

Carmelita had no idea what was happening, and began crying with her mom. Even as a baby, she could sense the tension in the air. Her emotions kicked in as soon as she saw her mom cry, and she wailed as frightened babies do. Sofía wanted to cry, but something came over her, and she held tight for her sister. Everything he was saying was worrisome to hear. Discouraged, she dropped her head down.

"Don't you know what our President is saying about *you people*? Didn't you get the message about illegals?" He had succeeded in scaring them. Another official arrived, and once again the atmosphere changed.

Carmen calmed herself down, but the same questions came at them again. This time, the officer took down the information on a computer. First they were directed at Sofía, then Carmen, then Carmelita: "You girl, What's your name?"

Sofía felt a nudge from her sister. She looked up and replied, "Mi nombre es Sofía."

"Where are you from?"

"De Guatemala."

"Why are you here?"

"Here?" she repeated, then paused, "Para acompañar a mi hermana...Sister!" She corrected herself, "My sister."

"Where are you going?"

"Nuestra Tia…Aunt Martina."

"Do you have any names? Numbers? Documents? Papers?"

Sofía didn't understand. He spoke too fast. She thought, *I'll just repeat her name*, "My Aunt Martina…Nueva York." She showed them her aunt's number, the ink barely still there under her arm. She was grateful it remained visible because she had so carefully tried to preserve it when she washed up at the last ranch.

Speaking in a neutral tone, he explained what was to happen next. He talked so fast. Sofía couldn't follow what he said. Confused, she preferred to remain silent. She didn't dare ask any questions in the only language she spoke for fear of more backlash. It was late; they were exhausted, overwhelmed, cold, and still very young.

He continued: "You will stay here in Arizona in a shelter for minors while we contact your Aunt Martina in New York."

She understood 'Aunt Martina' and 'New York.' Sofía watched his mouth move and heard the sounds coming out but she did not process much.

He related the process in such haste. There were almost no pauses in his speech as he rambled, "It depends on how long it will take for your aunt to respond with all the paperwork to be able to tell you how long you will be in that shelter. Once you are relocated to New York, you will have to go to school. You will have to behave, and begin a career, and then try to get a green card. Of course, you will have to go to court, and the judge will ask you lots of questions. He will then say if you could stay or go."

She understood 'school.'

He called Carmen next and repeated the information with her and Carmelita while Sofía sat still and watched. The room was getting colder as time passed. The men had taken all their jackets and belongings earlier and put them in a locker behind one of those rooms with a door. They were not used to such coldness. Once the paperwork was complete the officer separated the girls by accompanying them down a long corridor into two very cold air-conditioned rooms. Their light summer clothes were no match for the temperature of the rooms.

Taking a deep breath, Sofía slowly allowed herself to face the fact that she was now separated from her sister and the baby. She worried where they would take her sister. She wondered how Carmelita would do having been sick, and now with no jacket. She thought about her age, *I'm getting closer to 16, that's old enough, isn't it?* She revisited the long walk they just took down the hall, imagining her surroundings with all the different doors and rooms one after the other—like a giant puzzle. *Perhaps*, she told herself, *I should mark exactly where I am in this giant building, in case I have to run out or find Carmen.* Still, she wondered, *Where are all the other Americans? The other migrants... Just us?*

Left alone for about three hours, there was another shift change. A new batch of officers came on to work. This time, there was a woman officer. When she found Sofía lying down on the cement bench in the room, she immediately became concerned. "Would you like to sit with your sister?"

The nice woman officer escorted her out of the room, and they entered the room where Carmen was. Sofía was stunned to realize Carmen and Carmelita had been in the room right next to hers the whole time. Nothing made sense.

The three of them huddled together, shivering from the cold. The cold air forced them to be creative. Utilizing empty cartons and empty boxes stashed in the corner of that room, they held on tight to each other to stay warm. They delighted in their resourcefulness.

Noticing that this room had a door made of glass, Sofía was in awe. *You can see out of it!* She had never seen one like that before. "Surely," she said to Carmen, "We should see someone out there and perhaps grab their attention." She got up and knocked on it, hoping to see if *anyone* would check on them, but nobody came. "We're being ignored," Carmen speculated.

Several more hours passed. She was not sure how much. She lost count between the rapid fire of questions and the cold air. There was no clock on the wall. Sitting inside a room, inside a huge building, she could not judge the time of day without seeing the sun go up or down.

Suddenly, they saw someone familiar escorted into their room. It was Jessica, the El Salvadoran woman and her little boy! Sofía and Carmen were so happy to have someone to recognize and who recognized them. Their conversation erupted. "Oh, what a pleasure to be able to talk in Spanish, sharing details on how you got here after we left the border hotel," Carmen declared.

There was so much to catch up on. Their coyote had also lied to Jessica and Santiago about an 'easy way' to get to the other side. And like Carmen and Sofía, they described how they were quickly dropped off when the police sirens rang out for them.

Jessica explained, "In his usual gentlemanly fashion, Santiago helped me over first, probably using those same two blocks of cement and the re-bar that stuck out. Then, he carefully threw my son over the cement wall. I, too, prayed that I would catch him as he fell, but I missed. As I reached out to catch him, we both fell back to the ground. His tiny body somehow landed with only this small swollen bump upon his head. Santiago quickly jumped up and over the barbed wire by himself. He made it with just a few wire cuts to his hands, arms and legs."

Jessica showed them a few cuts she received from the wired thorns. They were nothing like Sofía's. As she recounted, Sofía and her sister listened in amazement. Like she and Carmen, Jessica had no idea from where they mustered up the strength to hoist their bodies over what they figured was a six-foot wall.

They concurred they must have gotten the courage from the necessity to help their babies and give them a better future.

"God must surely be repaying Santiago for his kindness to protect us," Jessica remarked. "After the men in the green uniforms questioned me, they didn't get me any soup! And they also took all my belongings—everything except the clothes on my back. They separated us. Santiago was ushered into another room and I have not seen him since."

They shook their heads back and forth and agreed, "Loving angels have been helping." There was no other explanation.

Food was the last thing on their minds. Between the frigid cold they were experiencing inside the room and going days without much to eat, they only craved two things: the warmth of conversation and to be on their way. Jessica wrapped her arms around herself as a gesture to communicate to the security guard on duty. She asked, "Please, jacket?"

The jacket she carried wasn't very warm; it was light for use in tropical weather. She was hoping to feel some clothing next to her skin. He returned but handed them one jacket—only one was allowed. So the three women and two babies shared the single jacket as best they could, along with the cardboard.

Later that night, they were tired, sleepy, and grateful to be gathered together with warmth from a familiar jacket. A patrol officer walked in and pointed to Jessica. He asked, "Do you want to go to your family?" They all sprang up in erect sitting positions.

Sofía tried to understand what the officer may have asked as best she could. She thought, *hopefully, maybe,* her family or her aunt had promptly replied to the border patrol inquiries.

He bent closer to them and repeated his words angrily and louder, "DO YOU WANT TO GO TO YOUR FAMILY?" Jessica leaped up from the tight huddle, grabbed her son, and that was the last time she or Carmen saw them.

Once Jessica was gone, another green-uniformed person brought them a green apple and a cracker with peanut butter. Sofía inspected it, then looked at Carmen and said, "I've never tried a peanut butter cracker before. From what I know, only children who suffer from malnutrition eat peanut butter in Guatemala. Do you think we should eat it?"

Carmen replied, "In this situation, I'm afraid. What if Carmelita or I get sick in front of these people?" So, they decided not to eat the peanut butter. They ate the apple instead. It was sour, but to them, it was real food.

At midnight, they called for "Sofía López" over a loud intercom. It startled her and Carmen, but Carmelita remained asleep on Carmen's lap. Sofía sat up.

"Come here."

She asked Carmen, "What are they saying? Did they just call my name? What do they want? Am I supposed to go somewhere? Where?" She motioned to Carmen, "Wait there, I'll be right back." She looked outside the glass door and saw a border patrol person waving to her to come out into the lobby.

She asked him what time it was by motioning to the man's watch. She could now see out the front door of the building and noticed the complete darkness.

He said in Spanish, "Es media noche." It was the last time she saw Carmen and Carmelita for a few more months.

Chapter Sixteen

The Baby is Gone!

Q. Do other countries have Amber Alerts?

A. The Amber Alert system is being used in all 50 states, the District of Columbia, Indian Country, Puerto Rico, the U.S. Virgin Islands, and 27 other countries. As of Dec. 31st, 2023, 1,200 children have been recovered thanks to Amber Alerts—131 of them because of Wireless Emergency Alerts.

Gunner's mother was cunning. Heartless even. She didn't care where Carmen had gone. She wanted her granddaughter back living with her son where she felt the baby belonged. Reina and Gunner needed a way to find out *where* Carmen had taken the baby. That was all they cared about. The problem was that Betina was still angry, held a grudge, and refused any further communication with them. By now all ties were cut off.

Bitter and infuriated, Gunner went one last time to their house to insist that Carmen's family members reveal where they were. Angrily, he demanded to know, "Where is she? Where is my daughter?" This time, he exhorted, "Did she go *North*?" Betina refused to open the door.

Gunner returned to his house and officially declared war on Carmen. Refusing to lose the battle, Reina raised her eyebrows and advised Gunner, "We're not going to waste more time trying to communicate with a family who is beneath us."

A common refrain permeates the small towns of Central America. It suggests that if you don't see someone you're used to seeing over a few weeks or months, you naturally respond with, "They went North." It happens all the time. One day you realize you haven't seen this person or that person around town in a while, so you presume they went north—to North America. As a rule, everyone understands what 'Going North' means. It might be your neighbor who you used to see out weeding his garden all the time, and suddenly you realize you haven't seen him around. Or the guy who used to hang out on the corner of the grocery store hasn't been around, one would immediately think, "He went North."

Reina decided the best way to confirm if her granddaughter and the wench went 'North' was to call on Betina's brother—her old boyfriend, Cecilio. She devised a plan with Gunner, convinced Cecilio would spill the beans. Reina would ring him up and tease him into talking, while Gunner would call Carmen's two aunts living in the US: Aunt Brenda and Aunt Martina. One of them would surely know where their young niece Carmen was hiding and hopefully divulge their whereabouts. The plan was hatched.

Betina was smart too. She made it clear to all her local family members, especially her brother, knowing he still had a sweet spot for Reina from years ago. She warned him, "Should Reina contact you, you are *never* to divulge information about the situation under any circumstances." Betina dreaded their revengeful threats involving the police, lawsuits, and bodily harm. She was aware that the law would not protect her no matter what they did.

Unfortunately, Cecilio never stopped pining for Reina despite the fact that their short-lived romance ended years ago. She cold-heartedly dropped him and cooled her friendships with the sisters Martina, Betina, and Brenda. The sisters didn't take Reina's actions toward their brother kindly and there began the bad vibes between them. Over time, Brenda and Martina moved to the States while Betina remained in Guatemala. Even though the women didn't move in the same circles like before, out of respect, they remained fairly cordial up to that point.

By now, a few weeks had gone by. The day came when Gunner dared to call Aunt Brenda in New Jersey, pressuring her to find out where his daughter and ex-girlfriend were hiding. Gunner insisted, "Did they go North?" Gunner kept repeating, "But I'm not seeing them. We haven't seen them." Instinctively they both knew what that meant. He was indirectly saying that he believed they went North to the US, possibly to stay with her.

Aunt Brenda was confused and concerned. She didn't know where Carmen and Carmelita were, but realized something was up. Betina had not admitted to her sister that she had sent the girls to cross the border. When someone 'left', one just didn't discuss it with anyone, not even some family members—that was another rule. Brenda immediately called her sister in Guatemala to investigate. Reina's plan was getting them closer to the truth.

In the meantime, like a small gossipy community where curiosity and old flames just can't die, and rumors grow like wildfire, Reina called her long ago boyfriend, Cecilio. She knew he would give her answers. Cecilio, of course, now had the excuse to speak to Reina. San Marco's triangular vine of scandal and slander grew deeper.

Reina insisted, "Where's Carmen?" "Where's the baby?" "Did they go North?" "It's been weeks since I've seen them." Reina prodded and teased Cecilio to tell her where her son Gunner could find them—out of deep concern, of course.

Cecilio knew but didn't want to be the one to fail Betina's orders. But…if he accidentally on purpose told their sister Brenda, then she would undoubtedly spill the beans to Reina, thus escaping the guilt of going against his promise to Betina. At the same time, by pleasing Reina, Cecilio hoped he could fall into her good graces, rekindling their romance. Blind as he was, Reina had intentions of revenge. She used him strictly to find out where Carmen and the baby were residing.

Family politics crept in and around the desperate long-distance phone calls. Aunt Brenda, worried, finally took it upon herself to find out for herself. From New Jersey, she launched into action. She called Betina, but discovered nothing. Betina's lips were sealed.

She then called their brother Cecilio and pressured him until eventually, he caved and divulged the details. "Yes, Betina sent them North." He didn't think he was doing any harm by revealing that detail to his favorite sister, all the while hoping he could score some points with Reina. He knew Brenda would communicate this to Gunner, and to Reina, whom he continued to secretly fancy.

Straight away, Brenda took out her phone and dialed Gunner's number, "Yes, they went North."

Enraged, Gunner barreled out of his house, heading straight back to Betina's house. Standing in front of their door, he screamed at the top of his lungs and threatened her with extreme violence. He was going to have them put in jail for kidnapping. He threatened to open a lawsuit. He threatened to put an Amber Alert out for his daughter, with accusations of neglect and kidnapping. He even threatened to have her killed.

Locked tightly inside her house, Betina was careful with her words. She screamed back, "Unfortunately for you, they are already in the States, and you can't do anything about it."

After much shouting and yelling back and forth, Gunner retreated to his house. Before he left, he shouted, "I swear I will get them back to Guatemala, and this will *not* be the last of me. I'll make you pay for this!" But the mystery had been solved and the secret was no longer hidden. Now they all knew the truth.

It took three more months before Carmen dared contact Gunner and confess they were indeed residing in the United States. She pleaded that he should forget about their daughter Carmelita for all the damage he had caused them. Of course, Gunner skillfully crafted his words. He lied and said he had changed, and that he would send them money to return. Gunner learned well from his mother by tempting them in any way he could to get what he wanted.

But Carmen saw through his lies. She told Sofía and their mother, "I think he is only saying things to get me back, so he can really do us harm for the hate he has in his heart."

Betina would remind them during their phone conversations, "Don't forget, he forfeited the right to have a family when he abused you."

Sofía agreed, "There is no way you can go back now. If you dare, you know he will harm you or have you killed. You have to stay here in the US for protection."

"He *almost* convinced me," Carmen confessed only to Sofía, "I'm unprepared for the life we've found living in the United States. I imagined it would be so different, so easy. Comparing my life there and my new life in New York, I'm wondering which of the two is worse." For the cultural shock Carmen was experiencing, she *almost* wanted to go back.

During those initial months since Carmelita and Carmen arrived in the States, Gunner attempted only a few more of his tirades at Betina's front door, unannounced, with claims that her daughter and granddaughter would come back to Guatemala to be with *him*. He threatened to expose her involvement with the coyotes to the Guatemalan Police and to have her arrested. He would yell at whoever was inside, causing a scandalous event for the neighbors.

Over and over, desperate for revenge and unable to declare defeat, the threats grew wilder. Gunner turned to threats of having Betina kidnapped and her other daughters 'disappear.' Eventually, Betina knew the intimidation and threats to call the police were baseless because they never materialized. She was convinced that Gunner didn't care enough since he hadn't carried through with the Amber Alert either. She ignored him and his pleas to get his ex-girlfriend and baby girl back and gave him no credence.

By now, Betina was impermeable. The constant intimidation just rolled off her back like water rolls off Vaseline. Gradually, the threats stopped, the pounding on her door, and the accusations stopped. Reina allowed Gunner to move on.

Chapter Seventeen

Temporary Shelter

Q. Where do children stay when they cross the border?

A. Wherever they are taken.

As a nice lady escorted Sofía outside, she explained in Spanish that she would be transported to a shelter for minors. Sofía didn't know what that meant, and her heart began to palpitate, her breathing grew faster, and her stomach began to churn. Reality set in for what she had dreaded all along: she was physically separated from her sister. But she did learn what time it was; the moon let her know it was very late at night. Two men handed her a small suitcase and her sweater, and in English, said "Get in!"

She got inside a border-patrol car waiting out front of the building. She sat in the back seat. As she looked around, she observed that each window was covered with iron. She heard the "click," and the doors were locked shut. Two officials, both men, sat in the front seat. Sofía sat all alone in the back. She felt sweaty all over. They drove for about an hour to reach the shelter.

Dios Mio... Dios Te Salve Maria...Padre Nuestro. Sofía recited three special prayers over and over in her head, just as her mother taught her in church. She kept her eyes open and vigilant as she prayed, hoping to keep her mind occupied and not think about where she was. She begged, *Please God, let nothing happen to my sister or my baby niece.* Once again, she didn't know where she was going. During the entire ride, the two patrol men spoke to each other in English. She didn't understand a single word. They laughed a lot and drank lots of coffee.

Occasionally, her mind went to the dark side. She contemplated. *Two men...something awful could happen to me! What will I do locked in here?* So many thoughts raced through her mind, but she knew she had to focus back on the positive because she was on her way. *Maybe they're taking me to my Aunt Martina's house?* She knew she needed to convince herself that all would be fine. Wanting to cry badly, she held back. Sofía did not dare call attention to herself with two strangers in a car. It wasn't long before the tears streamed down as she sat motionless, perfectly frozen. Not a muscle moved on her face.

The car finally stopped. They had arrived. She cleaned up her face and wiped away the tears before they could notice. A young lady came out to receive her at the front door and ushered her into the shelter. She inquired, "Como te llamas?"

Sofía heard the car drive away. She was afraid to look back as she took a deep sigh of temporary relief. But she also heard Spanish...The nice lady spoke Spanish and handed her another green apple, juice, water, and a peanut butter and jelly sandwich! By now, she was voraciously hungry and ate it all—still not knowing what peanut butter was.

The young lady, Terry, spoke slowly and carefully as she pointed to some clothing. She explained what was going to happen over the next month or two.

"Number one, you will stay here until your aunt completes all the necessary documents, then you'll be transferred. Number two, you'll get cleaned up and receive some clean clothes: a uniform of two pants and four shirts, underwear, bras, slippers. Number three, you'll share a room with three girls of more or less your same age, around 14-16 years old. And number four, you will attend school while staying here."

Finally, things were making sense. Sofía couldn't wait any longer and asked Terry, "Do you know where my sister is?"

"Since Carmen is around eighteen years old, a mom with a baby, she will be sent to a different shelter with similar circumstances." After a pause she continued, "Each case is different; she won't come here because she is a single mom, so unfortunately, she'll go to a different location and you won't be able to speak with her."

Sofía was so scared. She desperately wanted to be with her sister. She asked again, "How long will I be here?"

Terry said with a warm smile, "To give you an idea, well, some have been here about four months."

Sofía burst out crying, "I can't be here for four months! I need my sister!" Terry reached out and gave her a big hug. That calmed her down.

"Don't worry. You can call home for fifteen minutes on Mondays." After another long pause, she continued, "We go by the minors' last names. They are divided by the days of the week. Long-distance calls are costly, so the time must be limited." As she hugged her, she explained, "Because your last name begins with the letter L, you need to wait till Monday." That made her feel better.

It had become customary, sort of a rite of passage, that as each new person arrived at the shelter, they would put their fingerprints on the cafeteria wall next to the children's break room. Entering the room, colorful pads of permanent ink were waiting for the new arrivals. Each child would douse their fingers, find a special spot on the wall to mark that part of their journey, and add to the hundreds of prints already displayed around the room. It was amazing to see such a beautiful and heartening tradition. After leaving her mark, Sofía found her room, took a long shower, and counted the minutes till Monday.

Being in a new place with a modern bathroom, Sofía was unfamiliar with the faucets. Nobody happened to mention how the shower handles worked. She did not know there was hot water, and just by turning the dial, you could go from cold to warm to hot. Back in Guatemala, most places only had cold running waters. This worked fine for people living near the equator. With a hot climate, she anticipated cold water during showers. But here in this shelter, she didn't know she needed to turn the knob. Sofía took her showers for the first few weeks or so with nothing but cold water. It wasn't until much later before she accidentally learned she could have hot water—just by turning a knob.

The anticipation of Monday was killing Sofía, but it finally arrived. She was allowed her fifteen-minute telephone call to her mother. The last time Betina had heard anything from either of her daughters was when the coyote called to request the second half of the payment due for successfully bringing them to the border. She had no idea if they had made it across. Cell phone usage, especially a long-distance call from Guatemala, cost Betina more than she could afford. She had limited contact with her sister Martina in New York, and there had been no forthcoming information, so calls were few and far between for them.

When her phone rang, Betina almost didn't recognize her daughter's voice. She cried tears of pure joy the entire fifteen minutes, "Where are you?!" "How are you?!"

Sofía could barely get the words out, "We did it! We made it to the United States. I'm in a shelter. Do you know anything about Carmen? Where's Carmen?! The baby?!"

Betina replied, "No. I haven't heard from her yet. I'm so relieved you made it! What happened? Tell me everything."

"Don't worry. Nothing happened on the way. I'm okay. They are feeding me. I have clothes to wear. I can call you every Monday until Aunt Martina gets them the paperwork. I miss you!"

Betina had a hard time responding, "I miss you too. I love you! I am so glad you are OK!" Neither of them knew where Carmen and Carmelita were. So many questions, and only fifteen minutes, once a week was almost unbearable for both of them.

Sofía's routine at the shelter was simple. Everyone got up at 7:00 AM, brushed their teeth, ate breakfast, formed a line with girls on one side and boys on the other, and went to school. Education classes were offered daily in make-shift classrooms.

Basic English and watching movies were the highlight for her. Lunch was at 1:00 PM with American food: cheeseburgers, chili, pasta. Classes ended at 3:00. After, there were snacks like crackers, chips, cookies, and always something with peanut butter. The minors could walk around the grounds and talk. Girls and boys had to maintain their distance. They were prohibited from touching each other, but they could talk. Dinner was around 7:00 PM.

Her nightly prayers were consistent. *Lord, I miss my family back home, my sister and my niece. I'm so very appreciative for the opportunity to stay at this safe, clean shelter while I wait for my turn to go to my aunt's house. I'm grateful to learn English! Even though I'm not accustomed to eating dinner so late or eating American food, I think the structure is good for me. I'm aware that I'm being supported—that makes me feel welcomed! Most of the people I meet here are bilingual or bi-cultural—fortunately for me, so I still feel a little piece of home! They treat each other well. But what I look forward to is the once-a-week phone call I can make to my mother, and the thought of reuniting with my sister. Please let my stay at my aunt's house be good, not hard like Miguel said it might be. Please make the time go by faster. Thank you. Amen.*

The next time she was up for a phone call, Sofía strategically asked, "Can I split my time: seven minutes with my mother and seven minutes with my Aunt Martina? I'm dying to find out about my sister Carmen, and I wonder if my aunt has an idea." She was proud of her efforts to troubleshoot.

"Unfortunately, splitting up phone call minutes is not the rule here. You will have to sign a paper to declare that you have asked to split your minutes, and then we might be able to allow it, " Terry replied.

During her first seven minutes, Aunt Martina spoke in a matter-of-fact, cordial way. "Yes, I have *indeed* talked to Carmen, and all was well, but she is located in a shelter for *single* mothers."

Sofía was too young to have ever met her aunt in person. Intuitively, it seemed like an awkward conversation...*but it's my mother's sister, so I should feel reassured. I'm sensing my aunt isn't as excited as I thought she would be.* That tugged at her, just a bit. *Everything is going as planned, just as Terry has explained, and I should be allowed to leave soon. I'm sure my aunt is as lovely as mom.* I *have no reason to think otherwise.*

Seven minutes later, Sofía got to tell her mom that Carmen was OK! From there on, she continued to call her mom weekly from the shelter. *It's just never enough time to talk, but I can't talk about anything negative. I must only tell mom the good things I'm thinking and feeling. I don't want her to worry. I can't.*

Sofía never made any lasting friends at the shelter. She was shy and introverted, keeping to herself most of the time. She felt silence was the safest way to be. It was the best way to obey all the rules. She did manage to exchange names with a few of the girls. They were mostly from Central and South American countries, but none came from Guatemala. Down the road, they promised each other that they would find each other on Facebook. *I'm not really interested to find out details of the lives of those I'm meeting here. I don't want to know more than I can handle. I assume they all are basically the same as me anyway...went to school, learned English, and got a job to work. I just want to know about my sister! My niece!*

One day, about five weeks in, Sofía spotted Santiago in the children's break room. He had just finished putting his fingerprints on the wall. He had been transferred from another shelter while his connections in the US were being completed.

"Sofía! How are you?!" They were excited to see each other. "While I was in the other shelter, two of the six migrants that traveled with us on the tour bus, but got off to go through the desert...remember? Unfortunately, they were caught and deported." It was bittersweet news. Nonetheless, it comforted Sofía to know that he was there with her and that they had made it that far.

Finally, the day came. It had been around two months of wishing and waiting. Interrupting what had become her daily routine, Sofía heard the big news on the intercom from a counselor who called her down to the front office. Everyone pretty much knew what that meant. Out of breath, she raced to the office.

The counselor looked at her and asked, "Do you know why you're here?" The counselor smiled and said, "You are going to live with your family!"

Grinning from ear to ear, Sofía definitely understood "Family." Thoughts of happiness ran through her mind. She jumped up and down, she clapped her hands. She could not contain herself.

The counselor said, "Once you are out of here, you will look back fondly and remember your time here. It won't be like your life in Guatemala. Life outside of this shelter in the US is going to be different for you. It will be very hard."

Boom! She stopped clapping for a moment. That last comment hit Sofía hard. She remembered what Miguel had told her, and she got scared. He had advised, "I hope that you get where you want to be, and all goes well, and that you don't forget your family back home if you make it through." She hadn't understood that advice fully yet, or what everybody meant when they kept referring to her future life in the United States, but she knew there was a heavy truth to it.

She was confused about the comments of "hard" and, "Never forget the life you left behind in Guatemala." *Why would I ever forget my country? Haven't I always worked hard?* She wasn't sure she wanted to find out what they meant, but in a flash, she erased those thoughts and let the big news sink in.

A huge sense of freedom ran through her body. She wanted to jump up and down. She felt pure happiness when she allowed herself to believe she would leave the shelter. She couldn't wait to meet her Aunt Martina. The anticipation had been building. She *could not wait* to be able to contact her mom any day of the week, not just on Mondays for fifteen minutes. She was dying to know more about where Carmen and Carmelita were. Saint James and the angels who helped them get this far would surely lead the way forward.

Deep down, however, Sofía knew what the counselor said was true, that she would miss it once she left the shelter. She hoped the counselor's warning of a hard life was not true. She hadn't spent any time living with her aunt yet, so she had nothing to compare it to. She had no idea what awaited her.

The counselor concluded, "Your aunt from New York has purchased a ticket, and you are going to leave tomorrow."

Tomorrow! Sofía imagined, *Terry said 'ticket', did she mean a ticket for a car or a bus? I wonder how I am going to get there! I hope it's like the last tourist bus that had a bathroom right inside!* That is all she had ever experienced. *I have no idea where I am or the distance from where I am to New York where my aunt lives, and it doesn't matter...tomorrow I will find out!* Sofía was busy dreaming about going and let the details slip by.

After meeting with the counselor, she returned to class and bragged to some of her classmates that it was *finally* her turn! Now, *she* would be leaving! They all congratulated her. There was not much to say to anyone except goodbye and good luck. Time zipped by that afternoon; lights were always out by 10:00 at the shelter. Tossing and turning, she didn't sleep well. Someone would wake her up at 4:00 in the morning to leave. Taking a quick shower, she turned the shower knob to "hot" with expertise. She changed clothes, leaving her uniform folded neatly on the bed. Her old clothes from Guatemala were already packed in a small bag for her to take. Seven additional people were also lucky enough to be leaving that morning. The sun was shining.

Terry explained, "One guide is assigned to each of the seven minors traveling to the airport today. The guides will bring you to the airport and then directly to your flight gates. Each one of you is traveling to a different destination, depending on where your relatives reside." Her warnings were serious: "The airport is full of people...*never* leave the side of your guide! You'll get lost if you do! If your guide goes fast, you go fast! If he goes slow, you go slow!"

As soon as Terry said airport, suddenly, Sofía realized *how* she would get to her aunt's house: on a real airplane! There is only one airport that she knew of back in Guatemala, and not many people fly. Naturally, she had no experience or understanding of them. *I feel so ignorant. I've never flown before and still have no idea where my shelter is located on Earth compared to my aunt's house, or how long it will take.* Nevertheless, a strange feeling came over her. *It makes more sense, though.* Her heart filled with emotion, and she exclaimed out loud, "Wow! I'm going on an airplane!"

That morning, she slowly let reality sink in. *I'm going to go on an airplane, something I've only seen in picture books.* She wanted to savor the moment she'd probably never have again.

The seven lucky minors got in a van, then a train, which took them directly to the airport for their flight out. Everything flowed smoothly. Moments later, she was assigned to a flight attendant who would watch over her during the flight.

The last warning she heard from the guide: "Don't leave her side. She will bring you to your layover room in Chicago. Do as they say. You'll get lost if you don't—stay close to the person!"

Sofía was too excited about flying to worry. She was not about to lose sight of her flight attendant guide. She watched the clock and kept track. It went by fast. Chicago was about three hours from Arizona.

Once in the airport lounge of Chicago, the loudspeaker called her name for her connecting flight to Rochester, New York: "Sofía López." But the problem was that they called her name with an American accent, and she didn't understand it was referring to her. Again, they called: "Sofía López." She still didn't hear it.

At last, someone walked up to her and, in English, asked what her name was. She didn't understand the question. The flight attendant repeated in her best Spanish while gesturing with her hand, "Tu nombre?" She motioned with her fingers and asked, "Are you Sofía?" Sofía shrugged her shoulders, and together they got on the plane. The flight attendant motioned again, "Are you going to see your family?" Sofía just smiled.

On the plane, she received food. Quite happily, she still didn't understand a thing. Any time the pilot came on, she jumped in her seat. Around her neck was a lanyard with her name, the flight, and the destination. That is all she cared about. When she landed, she was met with someone in Rochester who spoke in Spanish and made her sign some papers to confirm that she indeed made it.

By then, Sofía's aunt had all of the flight information and knew where to go to get her. The shelter confirmed that her aunt would be in the airport lobby waiting upon arrival. When Sofía walked through the gate, she immediately spotted Carmen and Carmelita. Their eyes met, and they took off toward each other. They hugged harder than ever.

Sofía burst out crying. "Hermana! Mi querida Hermana!" She held on so tight. It would have been impossible to disunite them. She was not letting her sister go.

"I had *no idea* that you were going to be here!" As luck would have it, Carmen and Carmelita arrived a few weeks ahead. They had only spent fifteen days in their shelter because of the baby. When Sofía finally let go of Carmen and Carmelita, she turned and smiled at her aunt.

Chapter Eighteen

Unexpected Life in the US

Q. Is the American Dream real? Is life in the US happiness in paradise?

A. Rumor has it that it's true.

Had Betina known the reality of the living situation in New York or how much her sister Martina had changed over the years, she may not have advised Carmen and Sofía to go there. They had not kept in touch as much as she wanted; long-distance calls were costly, people got busy, and priorities shifted when family was out of sight. Between their respective economic situations and the passing years, their relationship had dwindled. Martina had escaped her own desperate situation many years ago and found her way to New York. There she had climbed up the proverbial migrant ladder, established a new life, and somehow became a permanent US citizen. Martina married a Nicaraguan US Citizen, and for all intents and purposes, they were living the prosperous American dream. At the time, Betina reasoned this was the perfect answer for Sofía, Carmen, and her baby.

Aunt Martina was accompanied by her four daughters: Amaryllis, 17, Daisy, 13, Iris, 9, Lily, 5, and one son Florian, 15. They were all named after flowers to symbolize their beautiful life. Together with her husband Franco, they climbed into their large van to pick up Sofía at the airport. Unbeknownst to Sofía, Carmen and Carmelita had been processed through the immigration system faster because they were sheltered in a place specifically attending single moms with babies. Carmen had no way to communicate that to Sofía, but insisted that she and the baby be right there to surprise her. When the airport passenger gates opened, they all followed behind Carmen. Excitedly, they took Carmen's cue and huddled around their new cousin, shouting first in English, then Spanish. "Hi Cousin! Hola Prima!"

There were lots of hugs and smiles, even though they didn't know each other. Carmen, Carmelita, and Sofía were the first Guatemalan family members who had come to live with Martina since she left Guatemala. The encounter with their new cousin didn't last long, and they quickly headed back into the van.

Aunt Martina wanted to treat them for Sofía's arrival, so they drove to Taco Bell for something to eat. Sofía didn't know what Taco Bell was. There were so many new experiences awaiting her, new places, foods, people, objects, vocabulary, and so much more she would learn in the coming months. She didn't know what to order and got what everyone else was ordering: "chalupas." These were very different from what they call chalupas in Guatemala. It didn't matter. She was famished and devoured them all. She was finally with family.

Aunt Martina lived on the outskirts of Rochester, New York, in a town called Ketcher. Her house wasn't near rural farm country, but it certainly wasn't in a noisy city either. *So many houses lined up right next to each other, so different from back home,* she thought, as they pulled into the driveway. Carmen grabbed Sofía's hand, and they explored the house right away. The five cousins followed behind. It was a long ranch-style with so many rooms! There were three bedrooms, a kitchen, living room, and one bathroom for everyone. It seemed like a dream home.

Sofía politely mustered up the courage to ask if she could call her mom using her aunt's house phone. Martina didn't have Wi-fi. She knew her mom in Guatemala would be waiting anxiously for the call.

Betina didn't know when but knew it would be soon, because Carmen had called her earlier that day and explained the news of Sofía's arrival. When Betina picked up the phone, neither she nor Sofía could speak. Instead, they cried out of sheer joy and relief. The love they held for each other left them speechless.

Sofía slept in a room with one of her new little cousins, Carmen, and Carmelita that night. The four of them snuggled in one bed. It felt just fine. Aunt Martina didn't have an extra bed for her, but Sofía didn't mind at all. She was content to be with her sister again. She was overjoyed to be able to contact her mother any day of the week, putting all her mom's worries at ease. When her head hit the pillow, reassured and happy, her face grinned with pure delight. New house, new climate, new food, new surroundings. She thought her life was going to be so good. Surely the worst was over.

Yet, she didn't sleep a wink that night or for many nights and months to come. It was the end of March, and it was snowing outside. Her mind relived the dinner they ate at Taco Bell and thought, *It's probably going to be a while before I can taste some home cooking like my mom prepared back in Guatemala.* Getting sleepy, she tried hard to fight off the intuitive thoughts and feelings that something was not right. They knocked hard on her mind and interrupted her rest.

There were warning signs right from the start. Aunt Martina's incessant comments she shared with a sharp, judgmental tone:

"When you come in *this* house, you have to take your shoes off!"

"When you live in *my* house, you have to put everything back in its place *immediately*!"

"*Here,* it's going to be *very* clean…not like in Guatemala!"

"Here, you are going to be well off, go to school, eat and sleep well."

"You can't make a lot of noise and run around leaving messes everywhere, especially Carmelita!"

"Carmen, you need to make sure *your* daughter doesn't leave any toys lying around!"

"You need to do your chores, help out and respect others who have done things *for you*!"

"You *will be* appreciative and grateful for *every* opportunity that has been given to you here!"

"Carmen will get a job right away, and *you,* Sofía, will go to school, study hard and get good grades!"

"You'll go to church with us, *no dating*, and lights out early every night!"

"You will cook your own food, wash your own laundry and keep your room tidy!"

Over and over, Aunt Martina repeated the rules of the house. Carmen, who had been living there a few weeks already, glanced at Sofía quickly and gestured to "just ignore her."

Sofía found her aunt's remarks puzzling and harsh. Although she was her mother's sister, it didn't take long to realize they were nothing alike. *Whenever my aunt speaks, it seems like she despises us and everyone back home.* She felt Aunt Martina was trying to change their minds about what it was like in Guatemala.

Was it possible my aunt could look down on us while she portrays herself and her own children to be of a higher class?" Confused, Sofía questioned her past. *Is it true Carmen and I have actually come from a lower class of Guatemalans? Perhaps our own mother hadn't told us the truth?*

I'm sure most Guatemalans value honesty, family, honor, work, and education...except maybe Gunner and his mother. My experience has been that people from my country are gracious and eager to find humor in situations, not like my aunt. She recalled, *In Guatemalan culture, visiting and honoring friends and relatives was important and meaningful.* Sofía ruminated over her aunt's words. *You will have to learn English! It is so much better here than in Guatemala! Your future here is going to be like a perfect paradise, because I'm going to help you!*

But what Aunt Martina *didn't* tell them was, in time, they each would have to work hard around the house, get jobs, and pay all their aunt's expenses back—with interest.

Sofía originally expected a paradise, a perfect life in the United States, once she crossed the border. That is what everyone said. Sofía believed what they told her. Everybody back in her small town believed in the American Dream. So young and naive, she accepted the challenge to leave her country, thinking it would honor her mom and support her sister who needed to escape. At the time, Sofía understood she would be able to happily go to school, work and help her family in Guatemala while living harmoniously under her aunt's roof. She felt the sacrifices she would make could give her great satisfaction and bring honor to her family, especially if she could send money back to her mom every now and then to prove she had made it. What she was learning was that the American Dream existed, and it might be the land of opportunity for some, but it was not the land of happiness.

Chapter Nineteen

The Blow Up

Q. How long can you live with someone before you have an argument?

A. Depending on your goal, having arguments can be a healthy part of any relationship. There is a difference between fighting and having a healthy argument. Fights based on winning and proving the other person wrong are toxic.

I don't feel bad about obeying all the rules or working hard. I just feel out of place. I can accept that Carmen and I are now living under our aunt's roof, and she has sacrificed to pay for us to stay. In my mind, having everything in the house clean and in place the way our aunt demands is a minor thing. My cousins are speaking to me in English, and I don't understand much, but I'll be speaking like them soon. I appreciate the hugs and affection I receive from my cousins too! She smiled, *Cleaning and doing*

whatever Aunt Martina insists on is a small request to get free English classes!

It only took about two months for a big blow-up to result. Aunt Martina first focused on Carmen. She relentlessly accused little Carmelita of her messes, the constant trail of toys, and an unsettling, unlivable disorder in the house. "She runs all over the place! Her toys are everywhere! She never finishes her food. She has no discipline!"

Carmen defended her little girl. "Sometimes little kids eat and leave the rest on their plate."

But Aunt Martina wouldn't have it. The rule was, if Carmelita left anything on her plate, Carmen was to finish the food. Period. "Nobody was going to be unappreciative of anything in this house!" was a common utterance from their aunt.

Sofía stood by and observed the comments, and how they stung Carmen. *It was unfair! Aunt Martina has her own five-year-old Lily, ironically doing the same thing! How was that unchecked?* Sofía looked around and counted the few toys that Carmelita owned. There was never much to pick up. It didn't make sense. As Carmen tried to defend her daughter, the tensions grew worse. Sofía felt it best to keep quiet and silently noted how their aunt treated her sister: shouting and complaining non-stop.

Carmen reacted differently than Sofía. She didn't hold back. She tried to defend her daughter. With fear, she said, "Auntie, what do you want me to do? She's just a little girl!"

Sofía desperately wanted to support her sister but was afraid to speak up. She tried to compensate by cleaning up whenever she saw something that might upset her aunt. Carmen's situation deteriorated fast because nothing was ever good enough.

Aunt Martina didn't assign Sofía any specific chores outside of the general rules to cook for herself and to keep everything clean and her room tidy. Sofía was never sure what that meant, so she always found something to clean in the hopes her aunt wouldn't say anything negative against her. Like Carmen, she was truly grateful for the food and roof over her head, even though in her heart, she knew that nothing was going to agree with Aunt Martina.

Carmen and Sofía didn't hide anything from Betina. They called their mom on Aunt Martina's telephone when she wasn't home. They told her of the shouting, non-stop complaining, and unexplained negativity against Guatemalans. However, when Aunt Martina called Betina to report how the girls were doing, she never mentioned the blow-ups. Instead, she would tell Betina that Sofía was going to enroll in school soon and was very happy living in the US.

Sofía and Carmen would sometimes overhear their conversation and just look at each other as they shook their heads in disbelief. Martina covered everything up. *Why would she do that?* thought Sofía.

For several months Betina responded to Martina's reports as if she knew nothing. But whenever she could speak to her daughters, she trusted what they were saying. She counseled them to "Try harder, just bow to fate," and "Have faith—Pray!" Betina would reiterate what her girls already knew: It was so difficult and expensive to get them there that maybe with some time, the dust would settle, and Martina would be more accommodating.

Within a short time, Carmen found a job working the day shift in a milk and dairy processing factory. They regularly hired migrants living in the area, many under the radar. Carmen would ask for a ride from new acquaintances at work, paying them from her earnings for the transportation expense. Aunt Martina and her husband both worked in similar factories, so she had no other way to get to work. Sofía would babysit Carmelita until she enrolled in school.

Aunt Martina took a few hours off from her job to bring Sofía to the local high school to register for classes. She learned that a student can't register without the medical checkup, vaccinations, and transcripts. All of this made her aunt resentful and fraught with stress. Sofía would begin in May, almost at the end of the school year. It wasn't much time, but it was the plan. It took close to two months from the time she arrived to get her school transcripts from Guatemala.

Even though Aunt Martina told Sofía she could eat whatever she wanted when she was home babysitting, her attitude made Sofía prefer to go hungry. She could hear her aunt's words in her mind, *What is this wrapper from? And these crumbs on the counter? Did you take something from the cupboard? How many did you take? Where are the apples I left on the table yesterday?* She felt it best not to eat or touch anything in her aunt's house for fear of another reprimand. She felt uncomfortable and unwelcome, like a burden—something she definitely was not used to.

Sofía reflected on the people she interacted with on her journey here—they were more generous than her aunt! Angrily, she thought, *It doesn't make sense why my own family would treat us this way. My aunt made a path for herself and her family. She has gone through the same path from Guatemala, to being an undocumented immigrant in this country, to her present status. She should be more compassionate and more understanding having been there, and done that...but instead, it's like she has used the idea of 'helping her nieces' as a bragging platform. She expects to be praised for this and expects everyone else to rise to her occasion. I don't get it.* With a heavy sigh, she acknowledged, *Yet, I am appreciative, and I will continue to get through by reminding myself of my mother's wishes and all Carmen and I have been through to get there.*

At bedtime, when Carmen got home from work, they would talk about their days. Inevitably, Aunt Martina would chime in and tell them to "Keep the noise down!" or "Lights out" or "I can always call immigration if you don't like it here!"

Whispering to each other under the covers, they would remember and compare all the noise, and the tropical, magical nightlife they heard back in San Marcos. Here, late at night, there was *no* noise, *nothing* but pure silence and cold, cold snow. Not a single car passed by.

It was a steady reiteration of the same...always a mention of "how much things cost," "money isn't free," and "You've been given opportunities." Even though Aunt Martina never directly stated they were not good enough, smart enough, brave enough, or family enough, there was always the feeling that they were doing something wrong or bad. Neither felt supported or motivated. They lacked both the external motivation and the internal inspiration they needed. They wanted to confidently believe that things would turn out OK. Sofía longed to hear her aunt say she would be successful and one day have her own paradise living in the United States, something she had previously believed to be true.

Things seemed to get harder and harder, not easier, as everyone except Michael and Terry had promised. Their English was still close to non-existent. Sofía would listen to her cousins blabbering away in English. She envied them. *How can Carmen and I ever get anywhere in life? Who would help us now?* That is when they began to deeply question why they came. By then, Sofía would continue to pray, but cried herself to sleep most nights.

About four months in, Sofía was finally able to attend high school. Carmelita enrolled in daycare right across the street. As usual, Aunt Martina would tell Sofía to "Clean this," or "Do that," "Go get Carmelita from the sitters until Carmen comes home from work." She always obeyed and prepared her own food as instructed. Carmen would arrive around 5:30. They had established a routine. Aunt Martina would cook for the rest of the family once she came home. Sofía cooked for her and Carmen. She just assumed it was her aunt's lack of trust in their ability.

One night, when their aunt arrived, she declared, "I can't take it anymore!" She was on a rampage. Sofía had washed dishes and vacuumed that afternoon, but according to her aunt, nothing had been done! As it happened, Carmen was working overtime until 8:00 P.M. Uncle Franco had taken their eldest daughter to Bible school. Martina was furious. She shouted at Sofía and accused Carmen of going out after work to sleep around with the coworkers she met. She went on to badmouth Carmen, "She's a mother of a baby. She's not doing anything right! Do you know where she is right now?"

Sofía froze, but knew she had to respond. "She's at work. She had to work late."

Martina declared, "No, she's going out to party after work instead of coming directly home. She is not attending to her baby and her future. You know the rules in this house! You know who she is with, don't you?" Sofía didn't know what to say, because she honestly did not know where the anger was coming from. But she did recognize the list was endless when it came to their faults.

Aunt Martina had worked up such a frenzy trying to prove to Sofía her accusations were true. She jumped back in her car and headed to Carmen's work. She wanted to catch Carmen in a lie—that she was really out partying, running around with men instead of working. But Carmen had already left her work and was on her way home. When Aunt Martina arrived, the people at the factory confirmed she had indeed been working, but she just left. Disgruntled, Martina turned around to go back home.

By then, Carmen was already home. Sofía had a few minutes to fill her in. Carmen was now aware of the volcano that was about to erupt.

Aunt Martina walked through the door, and the accusations began flying. Carmen tried hard to defend herself. "I'm working hard to pay off my debt to you, my mother, and to pay the babysitter. I even have to pay a co-worker to give me rides to work. I'm doing my best!" Carmen had never seen this angry side of her aunt before. Her aunt's face was red and contorted, her eyebrows tight with squinting eyes.

At one point, Martina tried to trick Carmen by saying that she had just come from Carmen's job and that her workmates said, "She left *with a man.*" Martina hoped to trap Carmen into saying something incriminating, and make her accusations true.

Now it was Carmen's turn to become infuriated. "Every day, it is a fight. You're never satisfied. Every day, you say 'Pick that up.' or 'Your little girl is going to stain our furniture.' 'Look at this mess!' You don't trust me, you say, 'Stop running around!'"

Tiny little fights every day, day after day, all added up for Carmen. So, she called her aunt out and said, "You're making this up! Let's go back to my work to prove it!" "Or better yet, call my girlfriend Lydia to confirm that she just gave me a ride home, and *no* man was in the car!"

Martina refused. She dug her heels in. For Carmen, the name-calling, belittling, degrading remarks from her own mother's sister were too much. She thought, "There's no turning back now," and confronted her aunt, sarcastically listing all her rules. Carmen informed her, "The rules, lack of compassion, and total lack of support make this house an impossible place to live or prosper!"

Aunt Martina responded by stating what both Carmen and Sofía had been feeling from the start. She said, "You girls eat here *for free*. You live rent *free*! You must mind all of our rules! You girls need money to pay off your debts! Carmen needs to support herself and her child on her own!"

It was obvious Martina had been calculating all along, "Between the flight, food, and the cost of shelter from just your short time at my house, I've spent at least $2000!"

She demanded, "Carmen, you *will* pay it back—*immediately*!" "Don't forget, I can turn you in to immigration and they'll send you back if you don't do as I say!"

Throughout this argument, Carmen had been holding Carmelita in her arms. Carmelita quickly went from happy to scared. It didn't take long for her baby's lips to quiver, then to a full-on howling cry of a frightened infant. Sofía was right there in the kitchen, observing and listening. As usual, she remained silent. She didn't dare offer her opinion. She didn't know how to speak up, but instead grabbed the baby from her sister and began to stroke her back in hopes of comforting her.

The screaming and yelling at each other went on like a tennis match until Carmen called her aunt a liar. She said, "*You* lie! Even if I was going out with someone, what's it to you? I don't want to be like you. After all, you are going out with a Dominican guy behind Franco's back! You are projecting *your* indiscretions on *me*!"

Shots fired! The metaphoric glass house was shattered. The truth was out. Carmen had openly revealed what *her aunt* had been doing. Aunt Martina became infuriated, so indignant at that last comment from eighteen-year-old Carmen, she hauled off and took a swipe at her as hard as she could across the face. She almost hit her, but Carmen ducked.

Martina screamed, "You wretched free-loader. You are not going to disrespect me!"

Carmen backed up, "You are not going to touch me, because if you do, I will tell on you!" That would mean big trouble for all of them.

Right then, Martina's middle daughter Daisy walked in and witnessed the scene. All eyes landed on Daisy, and they instantly stopped fighting. It was as if the bell from the boxing ring had sounded. Carmen went to her room to cry while Sofía carried the baby and accompanied her to their shared bedroom.

After a twelve-hour shift at work, Carmen still hadn't eaten all day. She sobbed so hard she could hardly take a breath. Finally, after a few minutes, she declared, "I'm leaving."

Sofía's eyes opened wide with surprise. She tried to talk some sense into her. They whispered so Aunt Martina would not hear them talking. "Let me remind you of all we've been through to get here," pointing out, "You can't leave! You have no one, no money saved."

"My work friend Lydia will take me in."

Sofía tried hard to rationalize that things would change for her, echoing to no avail how they've come so far and risked their lives—all for a better life. "You can't leave me here alone!" she pleaded.

Carmen wiped her tears, looked at Sofía, and said, "Go with me!"

Thinking ahead, Sofía was still traumatized and fearful about immigration sending her back. Martina had put a lot of fear into her brain over these last few months. She didn't know the laws in New York. She didn't know what was right, as the voice of their older sister in Guatemala rang in her head, *When in doubt, don't.*

Sofía was too afraid and perhaps still too young, to dream of a better life elsewhere or go against her aunt. She wondered if focusing on their shared objectives was more important than going against them. Ultimately, as one of the first decisions Sofía made in her transition from Guatemala, she courageously decided it was safer to stay with Martina and let Carmen go on with her plan. The only thing that stuck in her mind like cement was Miguel's departing words: "I hope that you get where you want to be, and all goes well, that you don't forget your family at home if you get to make it through."

Chapter Twenty

Time to Move On

Q. When is it time to move on?

A. The truth is, timing does not make a difficult decision any easier—clarity does. When trust and respect are broken, it is time.

Around 10:00 that night, another one of Carmen's work-friends went to pick her up. Carmen had gotten all of Carmelita's things together. They didn't have a lot. Sofía sadly watched. "Please don't go! *Please* don't go!" she begged.

Carmen replied in a whisper, "Do you want to live here like this? Can you? Do you want her controlling you all the time? Can you live with the constant threats that she'll turn us in? No! I'm not going to live here like this under her strict rules. She is just too unforgiving, mean, and judgmental! She doesn't understand. She has forgotten what it is like. She has forgotten who her family is back home. Her standards and her values are *not ours*. Her own daughters are treated like princesses, her son like a prince. They can do no wrong. We are treated like 'nobodies' in her house. There is no compassion or empathy. She doesn't really care about us. All she wants is somebody to yell at, pay her bills, and take credit for *supposedly* helping us out. We are not supported here. There's a better life out there, and I'm going to find it, for me and my daughter! I'm going to make our mother proud!"

Later that night, around 11:00, Uncle Franco returned from taking the oldest daughter to Bible school in Rochester. It was about a forty-five-minute drive from their house. As soon as they walked through the door, Martina told Franco what had transpired that evening, everything *except* the part about the Dominican guy.

Without knocking, the two of them walked right into the bedroom to talk with Carmen about her outburst and reiterate their rule about men. Immediately they saw that she had gone. Sofía lay there with her back turned to them. Her eyes were closed. She was scared to death to roll over and address them, so she kept her eyes shut tight, and faked like she was sleeping.

In unison, Aunt Martina and Uncle Franco yelled at her to get up. "Where is she?" they demanded. It did not take long before Martina called Sofía a liar, "*like your mother!*"

Finally, some things began to make sense. Sofia concluded that her mom and Martina must not have gotten along when they were younger, and now that they have lived apart for so long, Aunt Martina has slowly disowned her past...her culture, her people, and her own sister.

She somehow found the words to respond to her aunt's accusation. So out they came, but in a softer tone, "You shouldn't be calling my mother, your own sister, a disrespectful name."

Martina went on, "Ungrateful! They don't take advantage of what they have and the opportunities I've given them!" And she and Uncle Franco stormed out.

Sofía remained quiet. As soon as they left, she got below the covers and called her mom. She spoke very quietly so no one could hear. Sofía cried softly as she wiped the falling tears. Betina asked frantically, "What's going on? Why are you crying? Why did Carmen leave? She's going to get lost there!" Once again, she was troubled by the events her daughters were going through.

Sofía recounted the argument between Carmen and their aunt, the miscommunication, the lack of trust and respect on both sides, especially what Aunt Martina had harbored. "Don't worry mom, Carmen left with a good friend from work, so she is safe. I'm still here. We will figure it out."

The conversation was short. Sofía then called the friend to check on Carmen, but Carmen didn't answer. She prayed to God again, and asked for yet another favor or two. She asked, *How can it be that this family argument feels worse than what I've been through on the journey crossing the border? At least on the way here, I had my sister and my niece by my side. But now, I'm alone.* And once again, Sofía cried herself to sleep.

The next morning, Sofía avoided her aunt and slipped out the door for school. She didn't want to remember or discuss what had happened the night before. Instead, she just wanted to pretend. Sometimes school was a temporary escape from the sobering reality at her aunt's house. *Something good will happen today. Maybe I'll learn some English,* she imagined.

On the bus ride home from school, Sofía peered out the glass window, lost in her thoughts. She thought about what living under her aunt's rules meant. *I don't want to go to that house without my sister!* She hoped the bus route would last as long as possible to avoid the inevitable. *Surely my aunt is going to turn me in and send me back. Surely I'll be going back to the immigration police."* She wondered, *How can I live without my sister?* It was hard to hold back the tears as she reasoned with the facts. She needed her sister. She missed her mom. She missed her home in Guatemala.

Taking one deep breath in, Sofía turned the knob and walked through the door. She went right to work. She cleaned the counters, picked up, and did any housework she could find to do, anything that might please her aunt. Up until that moment, neither she nor Carmen had been allowed to cook for the family, only for themselves. They always remained separate from the rest. Sofía didn't want to be separate anymore. She supposed this was to keep track of the food they ate. But when Martina came home that night, her anger turned toward Sofía. Now that Carmen had gone, she felt like she was the brunt of all the resentment and misery her aunt held for them.

Her first comments were, "You're big enough to cook now! Why wasn't food ready when I got home?" Aunt Martina now demanded that she cook, but didn't teach her how she wanted things prepared. *Was this on purpose? Was this a trap so she can be right again?* Her daughters were also standing around, but all the comments were for Sofía. She knew it was coming, so she prepared for the worst.

Martina continued, "I'm tired. I worked all day and would like a meal when I get home!"

As her aunt rambled on, Sofía stared at her and considered what she had been saying. *Martina boasts about being the only one of the family who has legal documentation as if she were a pedigree. She flaunts the fact that she is a legal citizen of the United States. She revels in the fact that she has a house and her own children were born here. She brags as if she were entitled, the only one from her family of origin who actually made it. She looks down on the rest of the family, as if they were stuck there with no hope. I don't know why she feels this way, but I know in every cell of my being, it's just not right.*

She remembered her mom's story about the one and only time Martina had returned to Guatemala to visit after she had received her permanent resident card—also known as green card. *Mom said Aunt Martina made a big deal about the visit; she came wearing brand new clothes with her hair dyed and nails painted. She acted like a queen, like she was the only one who 'escaped' life in San Marcos. I was a baby, so I don't remember. But from what I'm seeing now, I can see what she meant.*

Sofía said nothing and continued to listen to her aunt. She didn't let the insults affect her like they had affected Carmen. *I need to prepare myself…with my aunt, something is always going to be wrong or not good enough. I'm still in this house. I still have a roof over my head. I still have an opportunity. I still can make things work. I can tolerate the rules here. I can't give in—not yet.*

Martina's treatment of Sofía, went on for two more years. Unfortunately, every day it got harder and harder for her. School remained a goal and an escape from her aunt's comments that she wasn't doing things right. Her English was moving along at a slow pace. The English as a Second Language class was her favorite because her ESL teacher understood how difficult it was for undocumented migrants. And in that class, she got to speak with other Hispanics. After school, Sofía continued to wash her own clothes, keep her room spotless, clean the bathroom, cut the grass or shovel the snow depending on the weather, and do all the housecleaning before Aunt Martina came home from work.

Secretly, she continued to speak with Carmen who was able to get an apartment with two other workmates. Carmen, ever resourceful and devoted to her factory job, worked endlessly to find a way to support Carmelita just fine.

Once a year, Sofía would report to the immigration lawyer to document how she was doing in the US. These required check-ins were crucial to increase the probability of obtaining her own permanent resident card. She depended on her aunt to take her there and help her report her progress in New York. She found seasonal work on dairy and corn farms, or working in fruit orchards. That made her enough money to send some home to her mother, pay back her aunt, save some, and occasionally buy herself something.

Carmen had disregarded her aunt's demands. Sofía however, felt more hurt than furious. She didn't understand how her aunt calculated any debt or wrong doing, because while she was living there, she cleaned and cooked and obeyed her aunt's every command. She justified the housekeeping services rendered should have been enough to offset any money her aunt spent on them. She painfully questioned, *What about the love of family?* Sofía endured the scolding and lack of compassion for her situation. She missed living with Carmen, but stayed with her aunt in the hopes she was doing the right thing...even though there wasn't much fun or enjoyment during her time there. The highlight was always when she got a chance to call her mother.

One day, she was in the strawberry fields when she began thinking about all she had tolerated and all she had repressed since she left Guatemala. She thought about the dangers, the risks, the excitement, the let-downs, the lies, the paradise she expected that never quite appeared on the other side of the border. She thought about her aunt's unwillingness to truly help them. She shuddered at the ease with which her aunt left her country behind and looked down on others and called it "supporting them." She considered the weekly calls she made with her mother and revisited the trauma she had been telling Betina all along. The time had come for Sofía to finally decide what she wanted for herself. The time had come to leave her Aunt Martina's house.

Carefully, she planned a departure in her head. The more she thought about it, the more excited she became. She felt liberated, almost tasting the freedom as she popped a strawberry into her mouth. Finally, she was ready to spread her wings. Now confident like Carmen had been years earlier, Sofía concluded she couldn't take this life anymore. Her decision was inescapable. She was tired of the rules—stated or implied. Picking fruit from the vines, Sofía had had enough.

That evening, she called her mom. She asked, "Do I have your blessing to leave?"

Betina replied, "Yes, It's time. Call Carmen and see if she can help you." Carmen told Sofía she couldn't take her in just yet but was happy to begin searching for a place where they could live together.

It wasn't long before Carmen found an apartment for the three of them. Carmen asked, "Are you sure you want to do this?" Sofía offered up all the money she had saved and was willing now to move out and create her own life.

Carmen warned her, "I can help you, but it won't be easy. You must continue to work and go to school."

Sofía called her immigration lawyer to make sure that leaving her aunt's house wouldn't harm her chances of one day being able to obtain a permanent resident card and live in the US forever.

He explained, "No. In fact, *you* could sue your aunt for verbal abuse if you wanted to."

She thought, *It doesn't make sense!* How different were the two worlds she knew.

Sofía was nervous, but surprisingly calm at the same time. As soon as Martina came home from work, she had found the courage to tell her of her plan to move out. "My suitcase is already packed."

"Your timing is perfect," Aunt Martina spoke calmly, "because it's at the point where you need to leave anyway. We've spent enough time and money supporting you."

She was shocked at how low-key her aunt's reaction was, and how happily she was to let her go. With no eye contact and not a care in the world, she continued, "I'm not going to stop you. If you want to look for your own destiny, then go, it's fine with me."

Sofía knew there was something strange behind this calm demeanor her aunt showed. But without wasting another minute, she called her sister. Carmen had one of her friends go and pick her up. With her new found bravery, head held high and looking straight ahead, she walked out—prepared never to look back.

It was hard for Sofía to work full time and go to high school full time. She worked the evening shift from three o'clock in the afternoon to twelve at night. That was ten more hours. She would get up at 6:00 AM for school the next morning and start it all over again. Not knowing English well, she thought she would not make it to graduation. Unfortunately, she left school, but with a plan to pursuit a certificate of General Education Development (GED) instead. She was so envious of her niece Carmelita, who was learning and speaking English beautifully.

And so it was. Sofía lived with Carmen and they had a small but peaceful two-bedroom apartment. Sofía found a better job in a factory with a bakery adjacent to it where she could work when the seasonal work ended. It wasn't long before their peace was temporarily interrupted. Aunt Martina came knocking and demanded $2000 from Carmen and $6,000 from Sofía. Aunt Martina insisted she be reimbursed for the lawyer visits, the $1500 cost for each of their flights from the border, along with the food and rent they incurred during their stay at her house.

Since that day, they never spoke like family to each other again. Aunt Martina barraged them with phone calls in efforts to collect the money she claimed she was owed. Sofía consistently worked at the bakery and supplemented that income wherever she could find a seasonal job at the various local farms. She was determined to pay her aunt back. She believed now she had a say in her destiny, and that her happiness in paradise was not far away.

Epilogue

Q. What is the difference between achievement and accomplishment?

A. Achievement is when you reach an externally set target while accomplishment means you've completed an internally motivated task, more for personal satisfaction and lasting fulfillment.

There are thousands upon thousands of untold migrant stories. Sofía's offers us a glimpse into a risky chain of events, showing the clear divide across the border where the grass was shining greener. It is also one that everyone can learn from as did I, the day she reluctantly shared it on the second floor of the high school girl's bathroom. Her memories reflect the pursuit everyone in the chain is after, no matter how small the link. She realized along with many others who chose this pathway, the journey was not as much about breaking the rules, rather having a significant life, helping her family advance, and doing well for herself, one obstacle at a time.

Ultimately, they were all in it together. Everyone in the link effected that change, no matter the deterrent, no matter a six-foot wall across the Southern Border. Hopefully, someday she can and will freely share her own story—the accomplishments and achievements—as it has been done here. Looking back as her teacher, a short article in her high school newspaper could never have properly explained her pursuit of happiness or how her journey showed us the power of situations and systems that were much greater than hers. Looking back, it is easy to see why it took so long for her to express to high school classmates where she came from. As a migrant, she didn't want to be bound to suffer and have limited opportunities. She simply wanted to matter, to have purpose, to be loved, to work, and to have the freedom to do so. Her story reflected that there is survival with change, risk, and a few lucky opportunities. It reflected how social networks bring about that change, albeit covertly. How many would have empathized or understood that without knowing *all* of her story?

Sofía had achieved her mother's goal of leaving a troubled life behind as she supported her sister Carmen and baby Carmelita. She achieved the very difficult and risky journey of safely crossing the US Southern Border. She accomplished the tasks of honoring her family—both in her native country and in the US—to the very best of her ability. She accomplished a forward move with her life in the face of all aridity, and she found her voice. Although she had yet to attain the coveted status of lawful permanent residence (the Green Card), citizenship would continue to be her target. Perhaps while the experience impacted some of her achievements and accomplishments, many other factors will also influenced the outcomes.

As hard as she tried, it was difficult for Sofía to totally forget about the situation she had left at her aunt's house, and therefore difficult to claim victorious. She blamed a lot on herself but couldn't justify how giving and doing her best could bring out the worst in her aunt. With the everyday stress of going to school and work, and being so far from her native home, something had to give. She wasn't sure how to finish her education but learned that no situation lasted forever. She convinced herself that this was just another temporary stage in her life and that she would eventually get her high school diploma going forward. She allowed her faith to lead her thoughts.

Fortunately, though, Sofía found a way to express what she felt and needed. She learned when to keep quiet and when to speak up. She learned when to obey the rules and when to make her own rules. Sofía now kept score and experienced how to advocate for herself each time she dropped off some of her earnings at her aunt's house. She enrolled in night classes to finish her high school degree. Her steps forward may have been small at times, but each one contributed to overall greater success.

Sofía's story blended her cultural heritage, and each risky unknown obstacle, into a personal history to reach the coveted destination. She observed intriguing coyote workings as links in an unbroken chain, connecting every movement of every participant within each step. The six-foot wall became a metaphor for her life's journeys, as she emotionally guarded the reasons why she came. She made it over even though she didn't know how to and couldn't see through. She was able to 'catch the baby' and move forward. Once she arrived at her aunt's house, she had to learn how to advocate for herself and cope with new definitions of what family means. Sofía had to come to terms with what her new role would be living in the US, and how to navigate more unforeseen hurdles, to ultimately accomplish what she came for. Her story showed how amazing humans are when they persist in the face of difficulties.

Crossing the US Southern Border helped Sofía and her family find the change they needed. It shone a light on the inner workings of family, the roots of the issues, the struggles, the sacrifices, and the chain of events that led to uprooting—and replanting—of their lives. She refused to wonder what life may have been like if she had never journeyed here, and had to come to terms with the fact that there was nothing much that her mother could have planned for her differently, because they both sacrificed greatly. She had to forget what she left behind and reevaluate her situation to move forward. She will always wonder if this is her final destination, or if there is a life of happiness in paradise somewhere else beyond the Southern Border.

Where Are They Now?

Gunner married another woman several years later and is the father of another baby girl. He left his work at his mother's shoe store and now works in agriculture as his main source of employment. He has almost no relationship with Carmen or Carmelita. Although Carmen allows him to occasionally contact his daughter by phone, they don't spend much time talking because little Carmelita doesn't want to speak with him now. Carmelita is healthy, happy and speaks perfect English and perfect Spanish.

Aunt Martina sometimes goes to the same church as Sofía, looking for more money. She declares the girls still owe her. Her oldest daughter left the house as soon as she was old enough, to live independently with her boyfriend—which definitely went against the rules. She, too, had had enough of the rules. She and her mother have not spoken.

Betina calls both daughters weekly. She has neither the money nor legal papers which would allow a visit, but she hopes and prays every day for that day to come and doesn't allow herself to dwell on it much. She is happy they are not in harm's way and have found their way in the United States. Betina and her sister Martina do not speak. She believes raising daughters smart enough and clever enough to find their way meant that she had done her job. Deep down, she also believes her children were not hers to keep, but rather to let go of to discover success on their own...that is the only way she can justify not living near them.

Carmen now lives in Ohio, with her Mexican boyfriend, who she met by accident at a friend's birthday party. Once Carmen and Carmelita moved out, they never spoke again with Martina, except to pay back the money their aunt declared they owed. She successfully reimbursed her with money she made at a farm that hired seasonal workers, all two thousand dollars. If she had to, Carmen would leave Guatemala and do it all again. She says she has learned she can provide for her daughter in the US and can give her daughter a better life not surrounded by the fear and rage of domestic violence.

When asked what was the worst part of the entire journey for her, without hesitation she said, "It was when I left the telephone charging in the wall and couldn't talk with my mom!" She felt so guilty alone in another country, jeopardizing their safety in a part of Mexico that was known for violence. Carmen feels fortunate to have a strong bond with her sister. She is convinced that she has the super strength to survive and resolve any future problems they might face, as they vow to always count on each other.

In 2020, **Sofía** worked extra hard and finally managed to graduate high school with a certificate for her General Education Development (GED). She did not complete the education she expected to, but recognized it was better than she would have done in her own country. Although she is relieved and appreciative that her English is progressing, she has only a few friends from church or school to hang out with who speak her native language. Sofía lives like many people, paycheck to paycheck. However, she paid her aunt back $6000 dollars in just two years and sent her mother money to pay back for the coyote loan. She continues to feel grateful for the opportunity to have lived with her aunt and cousins.

Sofía hasn't yet been able to share much of her experiences with the people she meets. She still fears that she must keep her past life private. Even now, it doesn't take much to trigger past memories, so she prefers to live in the present. She shudders to think, if she were ever asked by a policeman for identification, how she would respond.

Sometimes she finds everyday life across the border challenging...She doesn't have a credit card to simplify a purchase she'd like to make from Amazon, for example, and must rely on close friends. She doesn't have a license to drive yet, and fears going to the dentist or doctor because her job doesn't cover much insurance. It's difficult for her to find the ingredients to make the food she grew up with, so she is adapting her Guatemalan chicken dishes for tasty American-style ones. She never became fond of peanut butter.

The best update of all is that Sofía's found the love of her life, Xavier. Xavier is from Costa Rica and he came to the US in a similar way as Sofía eight years ago. He has a work visa and is employed by a construction contractor. They met at church and two years later had a beautiful wedding ceremony. Although technically their marriage remains unofficial, Sofía wants to show the world that she is committed to him and her life here, as they await her green card. Neither Aunt Martina nor her cousins were invited.

For now, they are not planning on having any children because if they do, and either were suddenly deported, they would be separated, and they could lose the American Dream for themselves and their future children, along with the life they have struggled so hard to create.

Sofía says it might not be the fairy tale ending that one would hope for, but she truly believes in the adage, *Truth may not triumph, but it persists*. Her greatest hope, her American Dream, is that one day she will be able to travel to Guatemala freely and be able to bring her mom here to visit the life she has begun across the Southern Border. When asked if she would do it again if she had to, she emphatically says, "Yes!" She now has a voice, a dream, a clear goal, and knows for sure she's laid the foundation for her future children who will surely do better—just as her mother did for her.

Discussion Questions

Themed Questions for a Book Club or Class Discussion

1. Love—What does love mean? How is it different from affection and kindness?

- How does love make us act—are we in charge of it? (Did Betina act lovingly?) (Did Sofía?)

- When do we show love? When can we and when can't we show love?

- What is the difference between love and lust as seen in

this story?

- Does love cost? Does it cost your freedom or your dreams? Are you free to love? How so?

- Love between sisters?

- Love between a mother (Betina) and a daughter (Sofía, Carmen)?

- Love between a mother and a baby (Carmelita) or a mother (Reina) and a grown child (Gunner)?

- Love between a divorced women and her old flame—can it change or does it remain the same?

- Love of a person who is pining for another—why does this happen?

- Love between family members who have moved away or haven't seen each other in a long time?

- Love of a scorned women who didn't have the life or the man she wanted?

- Love of a man toward a woman he really doesn't like-can this be love?

- Love for your country—what is patriotism?

2. Change—What does change mean?

- When do people change, evolve, or grow up? Under what circumstances?

- Are people free to change?

- Does freedom cause change? Are you free if you stay true to yourself?

- Did Sofía change?

- Did Carmen change?

- Once Martina left her country, did she change or was she repeating, recycling some of the same tendencies in her new country?

- Can you ever change your culture? Can you ever forget your culture?

- Will the taxi driver, Gunner, Reina, or any of the others change?

- Will/can a country change?

- How did the change in migration change a country? Change the people? Change outcomes?

- When you change the way you look at things, the

things you look at change…true?

3. Rules—Why do we have rules? Who benefits?

- When should we obey the rules? When should we break the rules?

- How do we know what is right and what is wrong? Should we believe everything we're told? Did Sofía believe everything she was told? Why or why not?

- Is it ever acceptable to bend a rule? Why?

- Is freedom a rule? Who says so?

- Was it OK for Carmen to leave without telling Carmelita's father?

- Was it OK for the tourists to not notify the Retenes of the migrants on board?

- Were Aunt Martina's rules justified?

- Did Carmen and Sofía have to obey rules? Did Edwin obey the rules?

- Do you have to always remember your past history, past culture, past life? Who says?

- When you become successful, do you always have to

help others to become successful too? Was Martina obligated to help her nieces the way they expected? Was she wrong to want to collect?

- Is it a rule to expect that you should help those from your same culture or from your same family?

4. Roles—How do people know what role they have in Society? In the family?

- How do people come to know their role in life or know to carry out their role? Who tells them?

- What does it mean to be empathetic, sympathetic, compassionate and/or unmoved?

- What does it mean to be human? Are humans free to be?

- What does it mean to be a link in a chain? How important is it that we know we are? Can there be anybody who is not a link?

- How many roles do we have? Are they ever defined?

- Is duty the same as role? Did the border patrol guards have a role or a duty?

- What role do myths, dreams, and goals have in our

lives?

- Did the ranch lady have an obligation to cook the eggs to perfection?

- Was Miguel altruistic or egotistical? Why did it give him pleasure to help people?

- How would you characterize the old man's reaction to the baby's cough?

- Was it Sofía's role to render cleaning services to her aunt?

- What role did authority have? Betina's, Martina's, the Retenes?

5. Vulnerability—What does it mean to be vulnerable?

- Are people born vulnerable? Is it a learned characteristic? Does environment make people vulnerable?

- Are power & strength involved in taking advantage of others, or is it the weakness in others? Was Carmen vulnerable to Gunner? Was Gunner vulnerable to his mother?

- Is blame a legitimate default for the vulnerable,

ignorant, or innocent?

- Are the vulnerable free? Do the vulnerable have a voice?

- Does bravery encourage people to be vulnerable? What encourages people to take advantage of the vulnerable? What should people do to avoid the worst-case scenario?

- Why did the Reten let Sofía go?

- Who took advantage of whom? Why? (Taxi driver, Retenes, Mexican Police, Guatemalan Police, US policies, Ranchers, Coyotes, bankers, diners, etc.)

- Did Martina take advantage of the girls?

6. Secrecy, Resourcefulness, creativity —How do these characteristics show up?

- How did these show up for the characters?

- Is 'secrecy' partly considered being 'resourceful'? Is it a learned trait?

- Are you free to be resourceful, creative, and secretive?

- Does dreaming enhance your creativity or does it cost you in other ways?

- Are these characteristics beneficial? Should we develop these? Or, is it better—even easier and perhaps safer—to stay in your lane and go with what is?

- How did Carmen become resourceful? What does that say about her?

- How did the driver know to fix the tire? What if he could not have?

- Was Betina resourceful or was she acting on another characteristic?

- The need to sew money in your underwear-was it resourceful, creative or should it have been a red flag of something else?

- Was it OK for Betina to be secretive about her past and her plans with the rest of the family? Was her secrecy with her plans advantageous or foolish?

- Should the migrants have kept secrets from the Retenes? Should the Reten have turned Sofía in?

7. Choices—What is the relation between a choice and a decision?

- Do you 'make' a decision or do you 'take' a decision, as they say in Spanish?

- How do people know when to make/take a choice? When to act?

- Do people appreciate having a choice?

- How does freedom, dreams, or goals relate to choices? Are we always free to choose? Why/why not?

- How are duty, obligation and betrayal involved with decisions? Did the Reten have a duty to turn Sofía in?

- Did Santiago have a choice? Did he use his instincts or was he taught?

- Did Martina have a choice to house the girls? Why did she make the decision t help them?

- Did Sofía have a choice to leave her mom's or her aunt's house?

- Did Sofía have a choice to speak up and offer her opinions?

8. Fear, being afraid of the unknown—How does this affect a situation?

- Is the unknown something to be fearful of? Who or what should we be afraid of?

- Does this feeling of fear happen only in survival mode,

under stressful situations?

- Does freedom, dreams or goals relate to fear?

- How does worry affect people's situations or
How did it affect Betina? Martina?

- How do people handle situations with and witho
worry?

- When are people anxious? Why?

- Are scary things bad?

- When are reactions justified? Were Carmen's reactions
justified?

- Were Gunner's reactions justified?

- How did Sofía handle the events in her life? The wall?
Her new life situation?

9. Motivation—To what extent do emotions motivate people? Are we always aware?

- What external things or events motivate us to change?

- Does money always motivate people to do things?

- Where does inspiration from within come from? How

under stressful situations?

- Does freedom, dreams or goals relate to fear? How so?

- How does worry affect people's situations or issues? How did it affect Betina? Martina?

- How do people handle situations with and without worry?

- When are people anxious? Why?

- Are scary things bad?

- When are reactions justified? Were Carmen's reactions justified?

- Were Gunner's reactions justified?

- How did Sofía handle the events in her life? The wall? Her new life situation?

9. Motivation—To what extent do emotions motivate people? Are we always aware?

- What external things or events motivate us to change?

- Does money always motivate people to do things?

- Where does inspiration from within come from? How

do we know?

- Is everybody motivated by freedom, by dreams and goals?

- Betina's motivation-was it justified?

- What motivated Reina more? Was it revenge, ego, envy, ambition, or something else?

- Was Martina bitter or helpful? Was she justified? Was she motivated to forget her past?

- How was Carmen's motivation to leave her home in Guatemala different or the same as leaving her aunt's house?

- What motivated Sofía to accompany her sister on a dangerous journey, yet stay at her aunt's without her sister? Was her decision overly influenced by others, or what she really wanted?

10. Survival—What does it mean to survive?

- Are success and survival related? If you survive, are you successful?

- How do people survive in situations? What things do they need?

- If you survive, are you free?

- Can you survive your own emotions or feelings or weaknesses? Can you survive your own thoughts? How?

- Does it take money to survive?

- Can people survive without love? Without family? Without purpose? Without a role? Without a job?

- Fitting men in the bed of a truck-was that survival?

- Did Carmen survive her relationship with Gunner?

- Did Sofía have to leave her country to survive? Did she have to stay to survive?

About the Author

Sally Doran grew up in a large Irish family and has lived in the US, Spain, and Puerto Rico. Holding a BA in Spanish and an MA in Teaching English as a Second Language, she is a seasoned educator with decades of experience in language teaching and cultural understanding. Career highlights include training in cognitive coaching and working for the New York State Office of Bilingual Education.

As a college adjunct, she has taught in New York (Columbia College, Le Moyne College, Nazareth College) and Puerto Rico (InterAmerican University, University of PR, and Polytechnic University). Sally is an active member of Hay House Writers Community and a Board Certified Hypnotist. Sally attributes her teaching, coaching, and listening skills to her deep understanding of the power of language. She currently lives and teaches in upstate New York.

Learn More

To learn more about Sally J. Doran and Crossing the Southern Border, visit www.sallyjdoran.com. For questions or comments, please email her team at sallyjdoranauthor@gmail.com.